ALSO BY KATY SIMPSON SMITH

FICTION

The Everlasting

Free Men

The Story of Land and Sea

NONFICTION

We Have Raised All of You:
Motherhood in the South, 1750–1835

The Weeds

The Weeds

Katy Simpson Smith

Illustrations by

KATHY SCHERMER-GRAMM

FARRAR, STRAUS AND GIROUX

NEW YORK

Farrar, Straus and Giroux
120 Broadway, New York 10271

Library of Congress Cataloging-in-Publication Data
Names: Smith, Katy Simpson, 1985– author. | Schermer-Gramm,
    Kathy, illustrator.
Title: The weeds / Katy Simpson Smith ; illustrations by
    Kathy Schermer-Gramm.
Description: First edition. | New York : Farrar, Straus and Giroux, 2023.
Identifiers: LCCN 2022055066 | ISBN 9780374605476 (hardcover)
Subjects: LCGFT: Novels.
Classification: LCC PS3619.M58928 W44 2023 | DDC 813/.6—dc23/
    eng/20221117
LC record available at https://lccn.loc.gov/2022055066

Designed by Gretchen Achilles

Our books may be purchased in bulk for promotional,
educational, or business use. Please contact your local bookseller or
the Macmillan Corporate and Premium Sales Department at 1-800-221-7945,
extension 5442, or by email at MacmillanSpecialMarkets@macmillan.com.

www.fsgbooks.com
www.twitter.com/fsgbooks • www.facebook.com/fsgbooks

1   3   5   7   9   10   8   6   4   2

For the seed

DRAMATIS PERSONAE

A woman, 2018
A woman, 1854

and, sometimes,
A ghost

The Weeds

Ranunculaceae

Clematis flammula, sweet-scented clematis

What am I looking for? Bipinnate leaves, a lacework root. The achenes almost fuzzy. Fuzzy's not a technical term— hoary, villous, sericeous. The lingo calls to mind the serious hoary villain who stirred his coffee with a scalpel this morning and sent me out in ninety-degree heat to inch along the stones of the Colosseum and scan for green while tourists swinging anvil-sized camera bags say *pardon* and *whoops*. My ponytail has been whacked to one side of my head. Find the plant, identify the species, check it off the list. Don't get sunburned; don't get harassed; don't harass anyone. Don't leave the Colosseum. How many people have died here? It's the tourists' Tevas that feel like the true decline of civilization, the all-weather nylon over tuberous toes, the dominant

3

species in this dust bowl. My fingernails are caked with the silt they shuffle up. Shit.

The flowers should smell like almonds, but all I smell is sunscreen and stench. To spot this first plant on my taxonomically ordered list, I only have to do a quick circuit of the perimeter, looking for massing vines in full sun, and then a half-dutiful scoot along the upper amphitheater, fiddling in the dirt for sprouts. (I'm not religious about this; sorry, science.) My advisor should be the one out here on his knees—oh, except he has tenure. I strike through *Clematis flammula*—she's absent, a casualty of industrialization, rising temperatures, the tourism economy—and wonder if the gladiators ever felt so trapped they might explode.

Anemone hortensis, star anemone

Rome without you is muffled; a wash of absence coats the stones. You thought my grief would swallow me, but lover, I have taken an apprenticeship in color: I mark down what grows, making notes so a man in a waistcoat can make a green and ordered story. Deakin claims to hold the keys to me. Not in four decades, he says, has someone combed for every plant in this great bowl, not since Napoleon put on his hat again and fled from Elba. I'd flee from here, but every other place I'd turn—my home, your bed—is barren. The Colosseum continues its crumble; the vines continue their sprawl. (The truth: I don't flee because you might return.)

Give me your faraway hand, let me put its soft skin here on this anemone: stamens and anthers of uncommon blue. Blue as oceans, as lapis paint, as the base of the horizon in heat. An early bloom. I inscribe a letter on the backs of sixteen petals: *Love, forsake me not.* There is no petal for the comma, so I leave it out.

In the ten days since you left, my breath works to fill the new hole. But I must have a man's conviction—like Napoleon, you'll sail back. The ancients thought anemones wouldn't open unless the wind blew.

Ranunculus, crowfoot
R. repens, R. muricatus

The sweat on my fingers makes it impossible to swipe on my phone, so I stop to drink, to lean against the same slope where some bloodthirsty pagan matron screamed for slaughter, to fill my stomach with cold Roman water that will find its way partly into my cells, ballooning them, and partly into my bladder.

I text my brother in Mississippi: "ALL IS FINE." He asks for proof of life; I send a pizza pic. I can't tell if he thinks I'm going to kill myself or someone else. He has wife plus baby plus managerial blah-blah. I have four limbs and a mean streak. If he thinks I'm chasing glamour, last week's pizza (€8) shows the height of what I've found.

Waxy yellow petals, short like schoolchildren. *Muricatus*

has a green center, making the plant look weedy. Too much green in flowers, and people think they should get dug up. I wipe my phone on my thigh and capture this specimen for my advisor. It'll live forever in my camera roll with several thousand other meaningless digital thumbnails: my face, sunset, plant, dinner, my face, plant, street art, plant, my face. A puny record compared to the old herbals, when leaves were stroked in ink on vellum. Deakin's 1855 *Flora of the Colosseum of Rome*, which I'm tasked with replicating—or responding to—had blooming color plates. He sat with his monocle and parasol and watercolors where I'm sitting, my shorts riding up, both of us cataloging what the soil could hold. He was the Bard of botany, the Crocodile Dundee. He rubbed *Ranunculus* sap on his skin to see if it was poison and induced *inflammation, and at length ulceration*. I shouldn't admit that I only signed up to catalog this colossus because suffering with purpose is better than just suffering. But there are many roads to Rome.

My dead mother grew buttercups. She pinched them off their stems and plated them for fairies. We didn't know they were toxic. We murdered a generation of elves.

Delphinium peregrinum, broad-leafed larkspur

The flowers shoot out on racemes like comets, like columbines, like dolphins, *delphis*. Their blue is thin enough to press and save. I should press them for you. Nothing brightens a letter like a bloom. This apprenticeship is a punishment, not a bravery. I have misbehaved—you, who carry the record of my truancies, must feel no surprise. My outraged father passed me to his friend and thinks I am contained: counting species in an ancient arena, kneeling to touch a rough leaf or bend back a weeping bloom, a woman left alone in public. The safest place is where all can see.

A profession is in some ways a marriage.

When Deakin explained my tasks, I was silent; as you would say, I showed him my belly. He gave me a tour of his Colosseum, pointing out the layers, the small climates, the places where light never touches and the damp spreads. He could not sit in the sun all day, he said. His work was not in compilation, but in comprehension. A higher science. "There is no room for trouble here," he said. He meant this as a protection, or a threat; a paternal tone holds both.

Before you left, I passed your new husband in the street. His eye was blackened from a fight, a smear of tomato on his shirt. I would have called it blood, but I know tomato when I see it. Imagine, choosing such messiness: a man, a marriage. But I'm here, stone-set, and you're there, boat-bound, both of us watching for dolphins.

Malvaceae

Malva, mallow
M. sylvestris, M. rotundifolia

Counting calyx, counting cleft, counting carpels. The British call it cheeses—"Look, Maude, a bank of cheeses!"—which makes me want to cram the purple bundles in my mouth and chew till I taste sharp salt. The petals are veiny, like old-lady legs. I have a field guide and two semesters of intro (physiology plus ecology) and a stack of articles my advisor printed out and my camera phone and a boredom that masks as persistence, so I'll survive.

If I had to sit in a lecture hall again, I'd set fire to it. This is my approach to life—identify the irritant, incinerate it. I knew who to attach myself to (someone doing research somewhere warm), and his boss put a stamp on my application because—I guess—I'm pretty, I'm pliable. My face when I got that email! My brother saw it, rolled his eyes, took his baby back from my negligent babysitting hands. "What next?" he asked. "Run across the Alps?" *You gotta settle*, he was always saying, shushing me. That was his nursery rhyme: *You gotta settle*.

The job's scut work: see whether this thing someone spotted here a century and a half ago is still growing (*Malva*? Found it!), and then my advisor will do the hard work of figuring out what these botanical shifts mean. (Is my generation the only one that can f-ing pronounce *climate crisis*?) He'll let me go at Christmas, when surely nothing blooms in Rome.

"Something is always blooming," he says. His mustache must tickle his lips given how much he licks it. His glowering makes me wonder if he asked his boss for a male assistant. I try to imagine being an advisor, saying dumb things, coming up with a project of my own.

If you're wounded in battle, the word on the medieval street is to find some bread crumbs and a mallow and mush them together and mash the paste on your festering sore. How often did that work? No wonder the fields of Europe have been made fertile with bodies.

Crassulaceae

Sedum, stonecrop
S. cepaea, S. gallioides, S. album, S. acre, S. reflexum,
S. anopetalum

I would crawl through a desert, starving for water, so I might come upon these ripe green bulbs and squeeze them in my mouth. Would they burst like berries, soak the tongue? You would say, my love, *Just eat the* Sedum *and find out.* I wasn't at your wedding but waited on the street outside, and when you and he came out with locked arms, your eyes were too busy to find me. He, though, met mine and winked, like a sated man wanting more.

Deakin asks what I know of plants—witches and plants are kindred, my father swore to him soberly—and I stand before his desk and say that I am attentive. His arms spill over the arms of his chair, and the papers on his desk look unbrushed. I have never met a scientist. He seems no worse than a jailer or a husband. He asks me to make sketches so he can check my work, why I am so quiet, if I have a suitor, whether I am afraid of goatherds, of skunks, of him, and in my dark gray dress I force a smile, just big enough to show him fangs. He gives me a botanical dictionary.

"Get home before dark," he says. "At night the Colosseum fills with thieves."

Did my father not tell him why I'm here? "They must rob each other," I say.

"List each plant you see," he says, rapping his thumb on his scattered desk. "Don't leave anything out. Posterity will judge."

They will only judge him whose name is attached to the work. There is a freedom to invisibility; nighttime thieves know. Though I would like to write a book, better would I like to lie in bed with you, the moths our only visitors.

My fingers find them growing sideways in the cracks. One *Sedum* is crammed in a niche where the lions paced; one crawls from the paving of a tiger's pen. The stone is cold. Touching a leaf is like touching skin.

Umbilicus pendulinus, navelwort

Succulents freak me out, like they're more animal than vegetable. I like my plants to shake in a breeze. These flowers are sweet bluebell tubes except white and pale, like naked grubs. Rub the leaf on your skin if it's irritated—e.g., if you're a nineteenth-century hay-for-brains and smeared yourself with *Ranunculus*.

This notebook says *Field Journal* at the top, which I interpret to mean *Private! Keep Out!* If my advisor ever paged through it, I'd have to find another career. I also have a field guide, a dichotomous key, and the internet, but still—half the damn plants on this checklist feel impossible. To what extent is my advisor messing with me? is a not-uncommon thought I have. Would he kill me if I went ahead and dragged a black line through all the boxes? "What f-ing luck, I found them all!" No climbing over this hot pile of rocks, pushing through the waddles of tour groups waving their flimsy flags, finding a crushed pile of stems and thinking, horribly, *I don't* care *what it is.* Data collection is more grocery shopping than science. Someone has to do it/anyone can do it.

"You're here to learn," my advisor said, "not to author." His basement office is like a zoo for stacks of paper. I'd just told him that we couldn't really define it as a European flora, given the number of naturalized species from Africa and West Asia.

"Is having ideas only for faculty?"

He leaned back in his chair, all white and tummy-round, and told the ceiling the history of his youth, the humility of research, the sexual thrill of submission to the academy. "One even *submits* a paper," he chuckled. I saw a crescent moon of flesh between the last two buttons of his shirt, like a cloacal opening.

I laughed along with him. Maybe he's right; maybe he's a swindler. My compass broke when my mother died. I run without aim, checking in with each man to see if he knows the way.

A Baroque doctor said navelwort "provokes urine," so I steer clear.

Rosaceae

Prunus avium, wild cherry

A sapling grows along the edge of the old battleground, barely tall enough to make fruit. The drupes are dark and small, following a white shower in spring. An angel tree, a tree of birds. Only its bark, striated, scarred by demon fingernails, reminds me of you, your back where the cat cut you. Cherry blood I had for dinner, until your skin was clean.

The nuns with their books look sideways at my hand on the trunk. It's late-summer warm, and we all have covered our heads. I cannot imagine this arena clean, filled with white sand, camels parading for citizens. It has collapsed into another of Rome's overgrown humps. We clamber over it, men and goats. There are places to hide, places to kiss. The benches burst with shrubbery. If I did not have my ordered task, I could get lost between farms and shrines. I had thought to find a way out—surely your ship has a sister— but the weeds prove better companions than the pall of my empty room. I can wait until I smell an exit.

The day you left, I was apprehended by a night watchman (vagrancy, intent to burgle) and taken to the city jail, where I was carefully felt all over—for weapons; for womanhood— and before my father could find me, the newspapers had. I was brought home in a shroud, my drawers emptied, your words found, sticky with the sap of love, redolent of theft. It was far from my first time. He paid the men so only a small notice ran: Unknown Woman Seized; No Further Plot Revealed. I can hear your silver laugh. All we did was plot. We drew futures out of nothing.

It isn't natural, my father said, his hands pawing your letters. I said nature made us both, and him too, and stinging nettle. I had heard of Sister Benedetta, two hundred years ago, who found Christ in another nun's body. And the teacher who taught English at the grammar school, who was whispered about, who never married. A thing being rare doesn't make it wrong.

My mother now wipes the scrape of cherry dirt from my cheek, and my father says my atonement won't last long; he's finding a man for his troublesome imp, and soon my acid will be alkalized. I have a biting sense of dread.

Pyrus communis, wild pear

Deakin says there are eight hundred varieties of cultivated pear, and I call bullshit. I've had maybe two or three kinds in my life, one that was soft and tasted like good soil and another baked at the holidays and cinnamoned to death. The unripe ones I like best; you can taste the potential—maybe it's like eating veal, if I were monstrous enough to eat veal. I left America because there was nothing ripening in me at all.

In Jackson the pear trees were the first to fall in a storm. They had a semen smell, an invisible rudeness; we held our breath walking past. My brother and I used to be close—or rather, when he sucked in his breath, popped out his eyes, I sucked in my breath, popped out my eyes. "Barf," he said beneath their spring pomp, and I learned: don't be delicate; don't smell like semen.

Pears to pears; it took me a long time to go nowhere.

I came to grad school for plants only because I thought they didn't move (they do), didn't have sex (they do), didn't hurt anyone (oh, they do). Now I tell people that I'm in plants because I like being proved wrong.

Like, I know there were trees in the Colosseum, that the purity of urban architecture crumbled into a romantic forest before it was wiped clean again, but a pear grove seems to be pushing the limit of belief. If there had been pears, there would've been jackrabbits, wild boar, roe deer, bears. Bears on pears—no Byron could've shouldered through.

Geum urbanum, avens

Buttercuppish. Before I err, I count: the leaves in threes, for the Trinity. The petals in fives, for Christ's wounds. Hand, hand, foot, foot, chest. You were the religious one, repeating what God would and would not allow. *This?* Yes. *And this?* No.

You were also the pilgrim. In a rare daytime meeting, you took me to the Villa Borghese, where we braided around the stone pines, brushing hands like schoolgirls. A man sold us candied almonds from a cart.

"I wish my wife looked at me so," he said.

"You should love her so," you said, and he pinched your cheek. Your boldness made me breathless. We fed each other almonds on the algaed stoop of a hidden fountain, and I pictured your skin beneath those narrow black boots, that frilled cream dress; your scalp beneath your golden hair.

"Imagine *him*," you laughed, "doing to *her*," you covered your eyes, "what *we*—!"

In the evening, I separate my sanitized notes from this field book and present them to Deakin. He examines my sketches and coughs phlegm into a cloth. His apartment is heavy with sulfur-smelling drapes, and I hold my breath until my thoughts splinter. The fresh air is spoiling me. "Your pater said you had an affinity," and I don't know whether he means toward you, the leaf, or the Devil.

Potentilla, cinquefoil
P. recta, P. reptans

A barbed, toothy, pot-like leaf, matte flowers in overlapping heart-shaped suns. I spent last night in an alley because I didn't want to go home, home being a rented apartment with no flowers, only a gas stove that lights my hand on fire every time I approach it with a match. The alley wasn't what you're imagining—no dumpsters and soggy cardboard, but a beach chair under a pergola of wisteria, where I covered myself with a dark blanket and imagined what my dead mother would say. (Not: "What an adventure!") I had outdoor dreams. I was not molested. My advisor didn't come and brush his bristly mustache across my cheeks. A kudzu didn't vine itself around my ankles and chain my legs. I survived my feral night, and when I crawled back into my cold apartment, I cried.

Rubus corylifolius, hazel-leaved bramble

The brambleberry only appears on two-year canes, suggesting that fruit is a result not of innocence but of consideration. Here in the amphitheater they drape over the top rows, where the bread sellers and priests are too shy to climb, and the berries go to waste. No; they are bitten before ripe by wandering goats, whose ankles don't mind the thorns. Today, high up, I take long strides, I point my toes till my calves sing, and I nearly leap, it feeling like love to move so hard against the world. The sun seems to shake in the sky; I feel sweat at my temples, along the lines of my belly. Who would have used this place to kill believers?

My first letter from you will release me. Some wiser in love would advise against waiting, but in waiting too can be riotous growth—look at these bucking brambles, who do not move but are not still. Somewhere on that boat you are writing me.

I find a blade, rusted but sharp, beneath one prickly rosette, from a lance perhaps thrown by a gladiator in a last humiliation. I hide it beneath my skirts that hide my legs, take it home, and place it in a box marked *October*, which is when you might return—which is when the berries, were they uneaten, would be ripe.

Fragaria vesca, wood strawberry

My ex would wait until I said something that reminded him of himself before speaking. It was like feeding coins into one of those yellow airplanes that bounce small children outside drugstores. I don't have exes anymore.

My advisor referred to me last week as "ungettable," as if it were a type. That night I locked my windows so hard. But I'll keep giving him the benefit of the doubt, given how universal my doubts are. We came to Rome together, on missions of promotion. Him to full professor, me to full human.

If I were a fruit, gettable, let me be a wood strawberry, which Deakin assigned a "superior flavour," "*more gratefully acid* than those which are cultivated." Emphasis mine.

Poterium sanguisorba, salad burnet

I thrill at my father's sanction each morning when I flee the house—why does he trust me to behave? He knows you're gone, and there is nothing left to steal except weeds. (All I'd wanted that night when they caught me was whatever you'd left behind. I'd grown lazy; I wore a white dress. In the dark, it screamed guilt to the watchman.) Deakin sends him regular reports—*daughter, present, pliable*—and my penance continues.

There is hardly anything passive about burnet—its bright balls of spiky blooms like hard dandelion puffs, its taste of cucumber. Francis Bacon planted it on his pathways in place of gravel so the high heels of Elizabethan ladies would crush the leaves and his garden would smell through the day of salad. What I know of plants is women's knowledge; men like Deakin study, while we inhale.

It rained today and smudged my notes—all that was left beside my sketch was *sangui-*, blood. The ink ran around it but would not touch it, like it wasn't blood but oil. Didn't you promise to write?

Agrimonia eupatoria, agrimony

He floats, a ghost, above the Colosseum. Drunk on apricot scent, his pants downy with burrs, the cloth buff-dyed. Common name, church steeples. He hovers over the women: the girl he ate, the girl who ate him. He counts the beasts who eat agrimony: snout moth, grizzled skipper. He has no pen in the grave. Everything he wrote has been torn from him; he has written nothing. Let the girls talk until they wear themselves out.

Rosa sempervirens, evergreen rose

Only one rose in this Colossus? After all that scrubbing in weeds, just a single white rose, once-blooming? It would be too ridiculous to admit a disappointment in an absence of love. That's not what I came here for. I keep my eyes low, ankle-level, not just to better ID but because it only happens when eyes meet eyes, all the shit and the fire. Build the moat. Keep the water high.

My dead mother too had a non-romantic vision—one year in a physics master's before my dad spotted her at a roller rink (this sounds like the fifties; it wasn't the fifties), her body smoothing over the boards to Midnight Star and Rick James. I wish I'd asked her if it was worth it. For one summer I thought her soul had reincarnated itself in me, and my job was to chase everything she abandoned. Or that was my excuse for trying LSD and punching a guy in the side of his head when he pulled up my shirt on the dance floor. I don't think it's immature to say I saw where love goes, and I wanted to go further.

That's what I need from my advisor: how to find a vocation without being a dick about it. He comes to watch me one afternoon to make sure I'm scooching just right.

"Don't forget the Porta Libitinaria," he shouts. The Gate of Death, where they carted out the corpses. Good for mosses. "Don't forget the—"

"What do you do all day," I shout back, "when I'm here looking?"

He circles around the broken seats to me. I'm crouching with a loupe in my hand. I'm not political, but I get a flash of what it means to be a woman in science.

"Interpretation is to data collection," he says, "as a sermon is to prayer."

I hiccup on my own bile.

The rose isn't blooming now. On one cane is a nub that's either a bud or a scar, and I take a pic and draw a sketch without color, just to make my hand move. Seventy years ago and a hundred and fifty years ago and a hundred and sixty-five years ago and two hundred years ago and three hundred and seventy-five years ago, men in aprons (I imagine them in canvas aprons, or maybe what I'm imagining are women) did what I'm doing: sat in dirt and counted carpels and drew bracts, all just to mark what exists—*exactly* what exists. Is that enough, to know six acres from root to anther and not a seedpod more? Not astrology or sex or the Antarctic or crime? That's not fair. Of course one of those aproned men knew about crime.

FIG. I

Vitaceae

Vitis vinifera, common grape

A heart-shaped leaf is my favorite leaf; I traced it on your forearm. You said, "I'm trying to listen." A quartet of strings under the window that opened into pollinated spring. Imagine not being able to touch a woman, when we were taught that women were made to be touched.

My hands run all over this Colosseum. I fondle every part I find—stones, shards, shrubs, bones—and think I could write the book of this. You would bristle at my infidelity; you would lie awake at night seeing my fingers twist stems that aren't yours. If you wanted less from me, I congratulate you on your husband. If I wanted more—why, I have gained a green kingdom.

A grape, like clematis, is a liana, and cannot sucker or

root along its lengthy vines, but must only climb, draping itself on any feature of its surroundings. It falls to the hands of scavengers with ladders, fishwives who come for midnight harvests with cedar pails and small scissors, small enough to be palmed, to be stuck in the sides of rogues. One of these women eschews wine; she wants to make raisins. She has no husband who would force her skirts, no children who yank for milk. Her parents died of plague. She'll lay out her prizes along the balcony in full sun, fanned by drying sheets, and sugar them more than any other human could endure. It doesn't matter; they're her raisins. This is self-possession.

Celastrineae

Euonymus europaeus, spindle tree

A stinking plant, fit for goats, which aren't here anymore. I consider harvesting some hot-pink pods to season my advisor's espresso—or would the stench tip him off? Called spindlewood because good housewives used it for their looms, it was hard enough and sharp enough to murder wool. In the sixteenth century, a pope tried to turn the Colosseum into a wool factory to give the prostitutes gainful employment, so their hands could stab at something softer. He died before the details were smoothed out.

Sometimes at night I list all the people I would murder, and damn, it gets long. Not murder, maybe—*yes*, murder!—but just meekly wish didn't exist, or I hadn't met. Those who have done me harm, who have pricked me and not reached immediately with their hand to press back the small drop of blood. One of my flaws, let's say, is forgiveness. Why give it? What does it give back? It's a negation of my original anger. In this psychiatric era, aren't we supposed to (though we don't) honor all our feelings? Or is anger not feminine enough?

I am practicing active thought. It helps me feel like the captain of my ship. I would actively crush *Euonymus* seeds into a cup of black coffee. Forgive me, tourists who look down and smile on a slender nymph with her passive box of pens. *Angel*, they think, *innocent!*

VII.

Paronychieae

Polycarpon tetraphyllum, four-leaved all-seed

Ground cover, with pink-green bells ringing along its hair in spring. It thrives in sand between the stones of the arena, imagining itself a bold plant, a warring Christian plant. My father calls on me today—or rather calls on Deakin—and finds me in the laboratory, setting leaves to paper. I hold the glue in my left hand. They tap their beards as they whisper, as if to remind themselves, *We are men*, and glance over to ensure I'm not eating the leaves or the glue. My father hopes a scientist can make rules for me, but this is a misreading of science.

If a woman ever asked how to find a calling, I'd tell her, *Investigate your own invention.* Perhaps she'd hear me and put down yet another man's list.

"Your mother has chosen a duck for dinner," my father says, examining my collage. "Promptness is requested." I ask him who the man is. Only bachelors merit duck. "A patriot," he says. By which he means a soldier, one of the radicals who dream of nationhood. Doubtless with black mustache and saber, a habit of using Latin phrases as if the language were a code invented recently. I have no country to fight for; I have only the soil. If I were a man, I would also have a house.

Deakin lives in an apartment with his blind mother above a butcher—he sometimes invites me. He likes his mother to hear a woman's voice so she can die in peace. I acknowledge it must be hard to have raised such an unhappy son, and if my presence soothes her, I am good at charade. She may mistake our discussions for lovers' talk, the way he blusters, the way I gently interject. How his voice diminishes mine.

Today I tell him of the allseed, outlasting a century's abuse, but he is only interested in the exotics. He has his theories about the Colosseum's bounty, a plant world created not by patient growth but by action. He writes about the species brought by spores in the fur and dung of imperial trophies: lions, giraffes, rhinoceri. A global flora, a conquering biome, a smear of masculine force on the soft belly of Rome.

VIII.

Caryophylleae

Tunica saxifraga, small-flowered tunica

Saxifraga meaning breaker of rocks, because its roots find the hard places to grow. I want my species name to signal breaker of bodies. *Corpifraga*.

At the dinner party they gave before I left, my father two whiskies in, my brother raised a glass and made a dare. "May you find purpose," he said, and his wife stood beneath the redbud, rocking the baby. The leaves sagged from the heat and drought. At some point in the next century or so, I thought, there will be a last redbud. Two of his friends milled around after, sneaking slices of caramel cake, making jokes about my journey. "I don't know, man, seemed like you really knew what you were doing in high school." Like I ever gave either of them a blow job. The baby wailed. Keep turning up the temperature, folks; my clothes may go and then my skin, but never my armor.

Tunica grew then and now, a testament to the longevity of stubbornness. It's been naturalized in the U.S., but I never noticed it in Jackson—or in Tunica, three hours north, where we'd go with fake IDs to gamble. Screw purpose, I imagine telling my brother; let me just get good at seeing things.

Dianthus prolifer, proliferous pink

When I was a girl, and before I was a thief, and well before I was a botanist's assistant, keeping my fingers in the beds where they belong, I had a set of watercolors made of crushed powder dyes. My favorite was the color that matched my mother's mouth—this was when she still spoke sweetness, before her voice grew opiate-addled and as distant as ships. In a night of sharing, when you and I had calmed enough to want things other than our bodies, I told you about these hues, and how I would paint on brick and skin and plaster, and it was you in your woman's shape—like a mother but not at all—who told me that the color pink was named for the flower pink, so-called because it looked cut round by pinking shears; only after centuries did they borrow its shape for a color.

"And what did they call pink before?"

"I don't know," you said, your legs sticking bare from the sheets like stalks. "Rose."

Romance is the bastard of simplicity. I should have started that night counting the days we had left.

Silene, catchfly
S. inflata, S. gallica, S. quinquevulnera, S. armeria, S. italica

The catchfly is an obscene little f-er, its stems so sticky that bugs get caught, and what was just exploratory starts looking amorous. How did Deakin describe it? *Pubescent, viscid, erect, club-shaped, membranous, hairy, deeply cleft, naked.* The god Silenus was the drunk one, the one who spit up, was covered in his own saliva. So too this pretty plant, flowers as naïve as phlox. How should it know its fluids are dripping down its legs? The flies know.

I was in Egypt when my period came unexpectedly—I couldn't have known—and I found myself in a toilet stall with nothing but a drain in the ground, my yellow skirt with a brown smear. I thought of the men outside the hardware store who would still be leaned in conversation when I came out again; their eyes having followed me in would soon follow me out, and my filth would find its way into their talk. Or it would be too shocking to be spoken—I didn't know anything about Arabic culture, I was only there for two weeks, in a writhing war with jet lag and a pale linen sheet while my ex took photographs of buildings beginning to crumble. Rotting sills, cracks in paint, vines coyly busting through plaster. It could've been Mississippi, but he called it

33

Egypt. You'd think he'd be more interested in my disgusting menstruation—when it came and why and why it didn't and what was lost—but I was just an American, like him. No art about it.

The Egyptian men noticed. What is the opposite of wanting to stick yourself to a woman's legs?

Sagina, pearlwort
S. procumbens, S. apetala

The pearlwort comes early, sprouts when sheep's stomachs are at their most echoey; the countryside rejoices when *Sagina*'s fresh green breaks through the late-winter fields. My Umbrian grandmother, who could name herbs at ten paces, let me hang it in the door to keep fairies at bay. Kissing a boy with a sprig in your mouth would lock his heart to yours. The countryside understood the need for love, even for shepherds and boys, even for schoolgirls' touches, if kept quiet.

Deakin said farmers' tales have no place in the manuscript. Again he showed me the order of an entry: identification, illustration, relation. When necessary, use. Not mystical use or ancestral, but medical, agricultural. There is a bias against time here, and I must fault science for its disregard of history. Does it think knowledge is not accumulated but sudden?

"Knowledge must be *current*," he said. "What we know is what can be seen. Write that in your little brown book."

I clutched it to me harder, wondering why I'd ever risk my journal in his butcher's garret.

Sagina was the plant Jesus stepped upon when he returned to earth, moist and bright, cushioning his stigma. Here near the south gate I lace my fingers in a mat of it, softer than the grasses. It holds yesterday's rain. Its prevalence is what guarantees Deakin's contempt. He would hate too the sparrows and the lambs.

Alsine, alsine
A. rubra, A. tenuifolia

I field-trip to the south gate of the Colosseum today, looking for the plants that insist on all the light. They root down in sand and wave their loose needly arms at the sun—*choose me, choose choose choose me.* I'm touched and embittered. My second-best friend in high school was a cheerleader who put no effort into self-sufficiency. And she didn't need to, not then. I didn't keep in touch; I can't tell you that she's a paralegal in an abusive relationship. Somewhere she's telling someone, "I can't tell you that she's a botanist's assistant, too liberated to fall in love."

This light feels sanitizing; it washes off the angst. Could anything rotten ever happen in a sun-flooded bowl? (Fine, I hear the thunderous rolling-over-in-their-graves of a thousand martyrs.)

I send my brother a selfie: sister smiling, sweating in

shorts. "Don't get too cocky," he responds. When we were growing up, I swear my brother kept a list of each heartbreak and accident like a debt I'd have to pay back. Now that I'm out of his hair—new digs, clean slate, fresh tan—he texts me like he's the one who's lost. "I need you to sink again," he wants to say, but failure isn't zero-sum. Find your own vocation, you nebulous mid-level project manager.

I close my eyes and touch the sparse leaves of the plant that's no longer *Alsine tenuifolia* but *Minuartia hybrida* because too many eighteenth-century men tried naming plants at the same time, and someone had to consolidate their egos. I breathe in, breathe out; consider forgiving my brother; and remember that nothing can be identified by sight alone.

Arenaria serpyllifolia, thyme-leaved sandwort

My mother served the duck in thyme. The soldier pushed it around his plate, unconvinced of its edibility. It might have been a sandwort—I can't swear she didn't forage in the Colosseum with the other fat women in black—but I drew it through my teeth and caught each fragrant leaf.

He spoke above all to my father, who spoke above all to him, and my mother's only friends were the servants, so I removed one shoe beneath the table and tried lifting it by the buckle with my bare toes.

After custard and pipes, he bid farewell by walking backward out of the house, clutching my hand, so that I had to be pulled to the door—like a queen but a queen compelled—and he pressed dry lips to my cold knuckles and made a statement about the vitality of the nation. I nodded. "Encourage him," my father said. "The history of the world," I said, "is a history of people searching for nations, and nations failing." The soldier looked to the other man for help.

Stellaria media, common chickweed

The yellow shell moth sends its starving larvae to chickweed. When they're finished being babies, they husk themselves and explode into bright yellow flying insects, wings marbled with cream and sulfur, shaky-lined, painted by a geriatric. I've never seen a yellow shell, though chickweed is common enough that most articles are about how to kill it. Imagine being a species, googling yourself, and finding How to Kill You.

I read a report that said more than half of women in STEM fields have been sexually harassed by colleagues, which is just shy of the treatment you'd get in the military. (Surely botanists are the stemmiest of STEMs.) One of the recommendations was *to diffuse concentrated power and dependencies in relationships between trainees and faculty/advisors.* Sure, okay. Or, easier, you could leave Earth. *Once I got into space*, the great Mae Jemison said, *I felt like I had a right to be anywhere in this universe.*

Cerastium, mouse-ear chickweed
C. vulgatum, C. campanulatum, C. viscosum

Everything but the flower is covered in down, like babies—soft, tender, exact. My mother had an infant late, and it squalled for seven days before quieting into a state that she called death, but wasn't. It remained quiet for a year, if you can believe that of a child. I wouldn't have told you, anyone of fertile years, but you're gone and can't be jinxed. My mother loved it until it became too alien, and though she dressed it every day in white and washed the white weekly in holy water, it never made another sound, not even an exhalation of gas. The Devil could not be cleansed away. She prayed over it, she let its blood, she pressed herbs against its chest, but she never loved it again. When it turned gray and dead, at last, none of us cried but felt like a chain had been taken off our chests. She opened all the windows and a lizard crawled in.

May a child like that come to no one, not your husband, not Deakin, least of all to a woman. Our duty is the preservation of life, but sometimes that means pressing our wet fingers on a wrong flame.

Moehringia trinervia, three-nerved chickweed

F- it, I can't tell the chickweeds apart. My advisor says the whole point of science is that you *can* tell things apart, but he's not sitting here in the heat, getting sand in his shoes and whapped by fanny packs, trying to tell an *Arenaria* from a *Moehringia* based on whether the seed has a wee white elaiosome. (And if it's not the season for seeds, God? *How shall I name it?*) That elaiosome is more than an annoyance to me; it also smells nice to ants, who come grab it and take it back to their nests, and tra-la, the plant has a new home. When it grows, does it explode out of the nest, sending ant bodies scattering? I picture those parasitoid wasps that lay their eggs in living caterpillars.

At our weekly check-in, my advisor says I'm veering too much into fauna.

"But it's an *ecosystem*, right? And if you're wanting a record of what's lost, maybe it's not just the baking sun that cooks things, but a lack of pollinators too, which you wouldn't know unless you knew—"

"I know what I need to know," he says.

I wait for him to laugh. He does not. "Where I grew up, you couldn't pick clover without pinching a roly-poly."

"You have an anecdotal mind." He's eating a turkey sandwich wrapped in a deafening cellophane.

"So when I see parallels—or things that interest me,

that are worth pursuing—I should just, what, keep my head down? Is global heating seriously not on the table here?"

He nods vigorously, lettuce spronging out of his mouth. "Of course these patterns guide the world we live in, and are almost provably true, but this project follows the dictates of empirical research: recording species first—the increase in therophytes, for instance—and only second making deductions about shifts in microenvironments."

"Therophytes?"

"Plants that die after reproduction and exist in their seed form indefinitely."

"It's just strange to me you don't seem to have feelings about the broader ecology."

"Feelings," he says, smug. "This is the problem with my female assistants—excuse the phrase."

Excuse the phrase?

"There's a rationality to science that has historically been associated with the male brain. Don't report me!" He crumples the cellophane into a ball and tosses it at the trash can, missing. "It's interesting, though, that some students still cling to a sentimental, or perhaps activist, mentality. I wonder—"

"Wait," I say, horrified by my own horror at being called a woman. "By feelings I mean ideas—senses—a larger context that we're fitting this data into."

"Ah. So your heart doesn't swell at the sight of the rose."

I squint at him.

"You don't intentionally wear this pretty thing," waving at my shirt like it's a mosquito, "to cause the swelling of hearts in potential pollinators. Men."

My eyes go big again. "No," I say, unable to say anything smarter. "No."

By feelings he means sex; by feelings I mean anger.

Linea

Linum, flax
L. strictum, L. catharticum

The former stands sturdy, tall, golden soldier spikes; the latter weeps. Strictness and catharsis. Breath and release. The gladiator and the blood. A spinning wheel in my great-grandmother's house used to churn flax, fibers becoming thread, but this Roman *Linum* is unspinnable. I sent a ribbon in my most recent letter to you. Silk from worms, not linen from weeds. What beauty comes from plainness. You complain about your winglike ears, and my hair is thin and no-colored; your breasts are too large and mine are too small; you have a short waist and I have turned knees. We cataloged each other into obsession.

I only wish there were more species here. That when you came home I would still be writing.

Cruciferae

Cheiranthus cheiri, wallflower

I know what a wallflower is; I earned the epithet plenty. Plain, brown, silent—the girl who stands behind the floor lamp at a party so even her shadow is in shadow. So what the hell are these things, loud splashy orange, as scented as a whore's perfume, provocatively, as Deakin says, *more or less stained with red*? This was the plant none of you f-ers thought to mention. They're practically nasturtiums, a flower my dead mother once tried to make into a corsage for my seventh-grade dance, the pouched mouths of which, as anyone with an eye for the pitiful could've predicted, wilted before my date took my hand. What do hands even mean to seventh graders. The brown mess matched my brown dress, crushed velvet, limp petals, clammy palms. I pulled away from him as soon as we entered the gym and spent the next two hours running from the erratic buckshot of the disco light.

No man gave me roses till my father, at my mother's funeral. As if her death were an accomplishment.

Imagine being fifteen and motherless and mad, a church filled with strangers in black, the sun cutting through the purple glass of Jesus's robes, and your mind on last week's fight with a friend. Nothing is real. Your pubescing body is suspended in a haze. At home, the roses smell unfamiliar. Your brother's door is closed. In the bathroom, your father is weeping. You cannot feel your teeth, so you crawl outside into the garden beds, tearing up the roots of everything she planted, waiting for your self to fall back into your body. There will always be a gap.

My therapist at the time encouraged me to use "I" statements.

Arabis hirsuta, hairy rock-cress

I creep within a fully jungled amphitheater, a detective beneath these clouds, feeling a quiver of discovery that my punishment was meant to block. These mysteries aren't unlike yours. Some species bloom, some don't; some have their telltale leaves gnawed away, and I must guess whether the residue on their stems is self-generated or remnants of some ruminant's cud. Neighbors hide kitchen crops behind wild shrubs, and specimens from Africa swamp the fairy gardens. Four tiers of terrain, not counting the subterranean hypogeum, the rooftop pioneers, the weeds in the sand outside—on the south side, if they wish to bloom. Deakin began himself, but paled the first day he went to his knees and began fingering the cresses. He is a muscled man, but not strong; he is British, after all.

Though grateful for my skill in his language, he is skeptical of the volume of species I report. I have carefully kept my notes of trivia on separate paper, in a separate language, waiting for his praise before I propose collaboration. (Don't envy my attention; this is a game I play to pass your absence.) I don't like the smallness of his eyes. I try not to narrow mine in return. At home, my mother in a daze asks after Deakin, says to me, "Be good, be good."

If I'd had a brother, would I have been better tamed? Did I sideways step into a masculinity—tender, though—because *someone* had to climb out windows, bring snakes home, hunger? Do species simply grow into the spaces they can reach? The *Arabis* shoots straight up like a white star, teaching me.

Cardamine, bitter-cress
C. hirsuta, C. impatiens

Picture a plant so sensitive, so f-ing heart-on-its-sleeve, that it built its seeds to explode in a shower of fireworks every time so much as the gentlest thrush wing brushes by. Here's how it works. A girl puts on her best underwear, lipstick. Goes to a bar. Stares soulfully into the distance, also keeping one eye on the game. No one is talking to her. Why is she at a bar. She drinks halfheartedly, listens to three women complain about their jobs on the gastroenterology floor of the local hospital. Wiping up more shit than usual. She fantasizes about meaningful work. A man asks to buy her a drink, but she can already tell it's a no; she says no. She's waiting for someone, she says. He rolls his eyes, bypasses the nurses, moves on. The seat next to her is empty for fifteen minutes, thirty. Her team is losing on the TV. Another man walks in, this one lion-faced. He glimmers. She wipes her fingers on the gin's condensation. She scoops her hair up and flops it to one side of her neck, then the other. She stretches her back, tilts her head, looks like she's been assigned a calisthenics routine to counteract early-onset arthritis. He is magnetic; he glides and simmers. He is the One.

It takes two minutes to make a fantasy. She puts words into his mouth, responds perfectly. *I don't normally* and *Of all the places*. He will love everything she loves, but in a better way.

At halftime, as she's writing her irresistible advance on a bar napkin, ready to slide it to him with navy-painted nails, a woman walks in. He stands. She feels her face turning red but can't turn away, can't be cool, not with her words already on this napkin. The man and woman embrace. Not as friends, but as *let me put my hand on your ass*. Their hips trying to fit into each other's, here, in this public place—they

46

have no shame. She has stolen their shame; she's drenched in it, it's soaking her shirt. Her redness goes white, the dream is tied to a stake and set on fire, and all the possibilities of her life are exploding like a sensitive-as-a-mother-f-er seedpod.

Sisymbrium, hedge-mustard
S. officinalis, S. policeratium, S. irio, S. thalianum

He floats, a ghost, above the Colosseum. He remembers fire—his own? No, the devil's year, 1666, and London was burned. From the ruins grew yellow weeds that rhizomed through the rubble, till the mayor—Bloodworth, yes, of course, not Lightgood or Boncourage—took to pissing from his carriage on the blooms. London rocket. That's what they called it—this mustard, girl, call it London rocket. See, she taught him history at last.

Diplotaxis tenuifolia, wall-mustard

The farmers' wives come in the morning to gather the first leaves before they thicken and sell them to dukes' wives for their salads. Gentlewomen must have ruder palates: *Diplotaxis* is acrid, tastes of metal and pepper. Everything in this Colosseum makes one's tongue twist, as if the bowl were a mouth, trying to spit us out.

Last year they tried with another bachelor, a man of law who brought his own fork to dinner. How could he have known I was a dark-eyed child, the kind who buried birds, who set the table with only knives? *She's quiet*, my father told him; *she's our meek mouse.*

My mother asked him about his mother, and my father asked him about his income, and I moved my finger along the table's grain, seeing rivers in that map.

"And you," he said, jolting me from some Atlantis, "do you draw, or do you play? Speak languages?"

"Everything," my mother said, her drugged eyes drooping with pride.

I was a year younger and knew that marriage required one answer of me. "Whatever you please." Their smiles were my reward. They returned to grown-up things, and I filled my mouth with vegetable pie.

I didn't have time to ask what salad you eat, but I have a memory of your taste buds. As smooth as something rough can be: like elm leaves.

Draba, whitlow-grass
D. verna, D. muralis

The seedpods hang out at forty-five degrees from the main stem like tiny green tennis rackets. *Thwack! Fifteen-love!* I pull off five or six to make a miniature tennis racket bouquet.

That's when a man drops a pencil at my feet. I take the time to evaluate it—black, unfaceted, eraserless, with a charcoal tip worn to a nub—before committing to a peeved glance upward. He's looking down at me, perplexed. Our expressions nearly match. I take his pencil in my left hand (my own pencil's in my right) and offer it halfway up. Reaching farther would reveal my armpit swamps; I play it coy. He drops his hand to take it. He doesn't accidentally brush my finger with his.

"What are you writing?" we say at the same time.

Normal people would've laughed, ha ha awkward, but we both increase the intensity of our expressions, and while I put a hand to cover my mouth, signaling what, intrigue?, he puts his pencil in his pocket, right where the fold of his hip is bound to snap it, and walks away.

I spend thirty seconds evaluating my own humiliation—why would a man engage and then abandon? Is it the zit on my chin?—and maybe another thirty slotting this into the patterns of my life. In miniature it's no different from a college boyfriend who loves you for three months and then loves your roommate. I am, we are, flowers to be alighted from.

I throw my tennis racket bouquet into the wind.

With my own pencil—sturdy, yellow—I mark a triumphant check next to *Draba*. I'm not a bee; I'm a contributor to world knowledge.

Iberis pinnata, pinnate-leaved candytuft

I once had a rabbit, a small gray bunny my mother had found with its leg caught in a poacher's trap, and though it limped, it wasn't lame. I carried it with me to sleep, where under the covers its heart went twice as fast, and I fed it from a saucer of milk at breakfast. It could only come outside when I was outside—otherwise, my mother said, the hawks would get it—but we would pick cucumbers from the kitchen garden together, and in the dusty path between rows of vegetables the rabbit left its prints: two small dots, and two long boats, one boat firm and one boat crooked.

The umbels of the candytuft are like rabbit prints: two small petals on the inside, two long ones on the outside, eyes of pink or yellow between. I don't know another flower with such a pattern.

Of course one evening I came in for dinner with a heavy basket of tomatoes, angry at my sister, thinking nothing but revenge, and I didn't miss the rabbit until bedtime, when my mother looked under the covers for it.

In the morning we found its prints as far as the edge of the lawn, two dots, two boats, and nothing beyond.

Lepidium granifolium, bushy pepperwort

Some folks used pepperwort to cure leprosy—which means they made some stinking poultice from a perfectly nice yellow weed and smeared it on the scales of lepers, and half the lepers died and half the lepers didn't, except *didn't they all die* eventually. This is my opinion of medicine. I feel like 5 percent of my life is spent reading the cascading studies about coffee or coconut oil or saturated fats, each of which disproves the next, in approximately seven-year cycles. Which I interpret to mean eat whatever you want for seven years, and then don't talk to anyone about it.

I don't know what food I put in myself as an adolescent except it had to be real small, both the bites and my body. If anyone had told me *don't*— Except I guess that's what I heard anyway. *Don't.* My brother's wife is like this, a nibbler, a baby rabbit, and he texts me that they're struggling. A wasp buzzes closes to my face, and I leap from one stone step to another. Yesterday some stinging thing dropped a tourist; he had to be taken out on a stretcher, clutching his elbow. Some days I smell a dark force here. The bloody scent of warrior flesh.

"Are you two talking?" Jackson is its own battleground. I can't imagine the bewilderment of a baby, how it sucks the self out through the nipple. I *can* imagine my brother turning his bewilderment into a boat and drifting away.

"I feel trapped." In his boat, as he paddles off.

"TALK," I text.

"Come home?"

Is that what's going on? He needs me?

Capsella bursa pastoris, shepherd's purse

I was called a weed when I was small. I grew fast and was everywhere and my father picked up his feet when I ran past, as if he might become caught in my vines. Two girls, each of us unwanted. Everyone waiting on my mother's womb to produce something of worth.

The seedpod of the shepherd's purse is heart-shaped and intentionally fragile; some call them "mother's-hearts," for how easy they are to break.

She eased herself out on an opium raft, her reasons more clear to me now I've been pressed through adolescence. Simpler to watch from a cloud, to keep one's smile. When I came home caught between my father's arms, the smell of jail still on me, his anger echoing, she took me to her bed and hid me in lavender. Outside the door, she met his shouts with whispers. That's when I heard—my head beneath her pillow—he didn't want to keep me. *How much quieter can I be?* I thought, suffocating there. I sneak, I calm, I touch, I kiss without sound. I think she had one victory left in her, and through her fog she won. "It was wrong," I heard her say to him, "but harmless. *Women* are *harmless.*" A common misconception: that because we cannot penetrate, we cannot maim.

She lifted her pillow from my head and brushed back my hair. "We'll find you a lovely position," she said. "Busy hands will help the sorrow." She identified me.

Senebiera coronopis, wart-cress

A spreading, minutely flowering thing; worthless.

I sink into a tub of water tonight, my head all the way

under. It's the closest I can get to being perfectly invisible—not even a robber popping his head in the bathroom to look for stacks of hundred-dollar bills would see me. I played this game when I was young, to see how long it'd take for someone to find me, but let me tell you, kids, this is not a game to play when no one's looking.

It has occasionally seemed, when I'm in one of these bathtub funks, that I've spent my whole life in this state, waiting either to be rescued or to drown. What a shitty either/or! It's f-ing hard to live. It's f-ing easy to be without sound underwater.

In my dumb imaginings, the people I've lost are floating out there in some galaxy, visionless and serene. The people I want to murder, though, *those* I'd set atop columns, naked, like stylites, their exposure maxed out. Oh, I would laugh at their bare bodies, and when they asked for food I'd launch them toxic leaves until they were shitting themselves. I don't think it's radical to say, in both cases, death can be justice.

Every three seconds a bubble of air shimmies up one of the hairs on my body. I am carbonated. I sit up like a baby being born, one great gasp at this surface world, but my head can't support itself—I fold over my bent knees, motherless. I feel on the edge of a fracturing, or a fatal drying-out. I need soil to put my roots in, quick.

Under the covers, dry, the alarm set for 7:00, I make a prayer for the wart-cress: May I find you tomorrow, pluck you, and cherish you. May you do the same for me.

Biscutella hispida, buckler mustard

Seedpods of highest interest, shaped like small medieval shields, or bucklers, of the kind held in one hand to deflect blows while the other hand thrusts about with the sword. Of course, they are also shaped like breasts, but the plant has escaped the designation "breast mustard."

I pressed some onto paper, covered them in shellac so they might last, and sent them as poor gifts to you, with the hope that they might resemble planets and the distance between us would thus seem smaller. But I've had no response; have you not made it to your first port yet? The soldier brought by a book last night—a pamphlet, really, for some ideas would suffer from expansion—and I sat next to him in the parlor, my palms on the horsehair. No touch was initiated. He tried to reach for my mind, and I said he was probing barren soil.

"I haven't the training," I said.

He kept his eyes on his knees. "Your father said he picked your tutors himself."

"My father would boast his way out of poverty."

"You'd rather not talk about the fate of capitalism. Poetry? Mythology?"

"I know no poems."

He looked into his lap. I could see the downiness of his ear and pitied him.

"Do you know of plants?" I said.

His glance told me the smallness of this subject.

"Then one of us must study," I said without a blush. And stood and bowed and left.

Bunias erucago, prickly-podded bunias

If Seuss wrote a Colosseum verse ("Fight, Romans, fight / Fight with all your might! / Go, lions, go / Grab them by the toe!"), he would happily illustrate the pods of the prickly-podded bunias, also called corn rocket or crested warty-cabbage, which scores an inexplicable 3 out of 5 on one database's edibility scale. Why isn't that a zero-or-one prop-osition? What on earth does "3" imply? The pods are spiked sultan's caps, the spikes in uneven, rose-tipped efflores-cences, like angel wings, or bloody rags in a high wind. I've looked from the hypogeum to the roof and never found a hint of this sucker. I've pushed people's Tevas aside, peeked in the port-a-potties, asked the ticket taker if he was hiding a seed in his pocket or was just confused to see me. It's not here, the wartycabbage. I'm let down. I tell my advisor in my weekly confessional; he shrugs. I don't like seeing people shrug. I don't like how it makes caterpillars of their shoul-ders, how my own skin crawls at their shorthand for apathy.

I tell him instead that I've found a specimen of *Coreopsis*. His eyes narrow.

"It's a joke," I say. Though I could easily have carried their seeds in my shoelaces from our native North Amer-ica and shuffled through the willing Colosseum dirt and accidentally spit copiously on them until they sprouted and bloomed, happy grandmother yellow. So what if it's not the same climate; nothing's the same climate anymore.

"I used to make jokes," he says, which is not what I thought he'd say. *Botanists don't joke* is what I had my money on. I'm wearing a big dark sack of a shirt today so that he won't look at my chest.

"What did you find funniest?" I say.

"Herpetologists."

I cannot imagine anyone having an affair with my advisor.

XI

Cytineae

Cytinus hypocistus, cistus cytinus

Some plants, like lovers, are parasitical. This one dresses in yellow-red, like the frock you wore to the book market the day you made me read John Donne aloud. The cistus does not process light into food like its green-leafed kin, but suckers to the white roots of its host and pulls its dinner out of its neighbor's stomach. In spring the orange blooms burst Athena-like from the soil, independent of stem or leaf, and those bulbous bells wait like a fungal growth for a beetle to trundle by and eat them. The beetle, lowly, obliges. A burrowing kind, it writhes down in sand or soil to escape the heat of day, and thus its dung is positioned half an inch below the earth, that much nearer another set of waiting roots.

"Listen to her fine accent," you told the vendor, whose

antique prints filled his stall with must. "Couldn't she pass for an English rose?"

You liked seeing others' admiration of me. I liked only you and wanted the privacy of night. "'Oh, do not die,'" I read, turning my voice curt, Northern, "'for I shall hate all women so, when thou art gone.'"

"The only woman you need is the woman you love," the vendor said, looking out toward the Tiber like a sea captain.

"Though sometimes, for love, you need more than one," you said, and he queered his eye, and I twisted the skin of your wrist.

Do not let me sucker you. Writing so often could seem like giving, but I'm cannier than that; I'm stealing your eyes, attempting to parasite your heart.

XII

Geraniaceae

Geranium, crane's-bill
G. molle, G. robertianum, G. rotundifolium, G. dissectum

Here's a botany joke: How do you tell a woman in her twenties from a woman in her thirties? The former has ten perfect stamens; the latter has five perfect stamens and five barren ones. Just kidding; that's how you tell a *Geranium* from an *Erodium*.

Called herb Robert, red robin, stinking Bob, crow's foot, death-come-quickly. All names I'd give my children, happily, darkly, names for them to outgrow.

My own dead mother grew red geraniums in baskets that hung from our windowsills. A neighbor who knew more than us called them false geraniums. *Pelargonium*, she said. "She can *pelar-go-away*," my mother said. They were blooming when she brought me home from the hospital, and they were blooming when I stole one of her black dresses to wear to her funeral.

No one waters the boxes anymore; there are no women to tend them, no children to crush their curly leaves with bare hands for the scent, though there are probably still neighbors to split hairs. (When I learned in Structural Botany that both *Geraniums* and *Pelargoniums* nested in the *Geraniaceae* family, that our stuck-up neighbor had been wrong, I had to leave the class to burst into tears because it was too late to call my mother.)

This sounds like an after-school special, but I feel like knowledge is the pair of sneakers that helps me run past her death—as if new facts measure growth that measures distance from the disaster. After a breakup, aren't you supposed to get a new hobby? It's not actually about growing; it's about changing yourself into someone your grief won't recognize.

Erodium, stork's-bill
E. cicutarium, E. moschatum, E. romanum, E. malacoides

Someday when the land's been laid waste, the Colosseum wrecked, my family still burning in the embers, I imagine a boat will appear named *Regret*, and you will take my face and recite the story of the day we met: the night. I must believe our world can do that, can keep turning itself over again.

The stork's-bill has perfected the art of birth. Its seeds are little machines for success: as they dry, a springing force ejects the seed from its parent, its sharp beak penetrating the soil. Here, according to the vicissitudes of humidity, the seed's awn—a spiraling appendage—expands and contracts, screwing the seed farther into the soil. On the awn's back are bristles that prevent any upward movement, keeping the seed tightly hidden. Thus is it locked in for the night, for safety.

I make a sketch of its pinched leaves and draw a faint moon above. A moon you might spy from whatever new prison you've made.

XIII.

Rutaceae

Ruta bracteosa, large bracteated rue

Deakin commends it for a *bitter and nauseous taste*. Was he humping along the rows of seats, sneaking seeds in his mouth? (I see him potbellied, bewhiskered, cravatted, definitely with woolen underwear.) What's the mortality rate for botanists?

Reading his musty text can give me the willies; like, I hear him and see him, but also see something else—something more feminine, curious, a kind of palimpsest. I'd ask my advisor, but he has zero interest in anything that smells of humanity.

Whoever went around noshing on plants, I sympathize, at least with rue, those leaves cool-blue, smooth. I'd rather put that in my mouth than arugula. It reminds me of *Baptisia*, as clean as a child's drawing, nothing hairy, extraneous. A plant that shaves its legs—expecting to be bitten. (*Baptisia* was one of the first to spring out of the soil in Jackson, just after our Tête-à-Tête daffodils, and I'd wait for its greenery like I waited for TGIF.)

I start shaving my legs again, in case the man with the pencil comes back. But who in his right mind would visit the Colosseum twice, €12 each time, ten thousand tourists each day? Not a man who carries pencils. I say I'm shaving my legs for myself, but I don't do anything for myself.

XIV.

Oxalideae

Oxalis corniculata, yellow procumbent wood-sorrel

Called sleeping beauty, tastes of lemon. While the beauties are sleeping, I creep. I began because I was young and had nothing substantial to occupy my mind. I needed nothing; I was clothed and fed according to the standards of the provided class. I had ribbons for my hair, in silk. But I was thirteen and the night heaved with risk and sin. The first time was my neighbor's house, its windows sagging with age, its owner white-haired and deaf. I brought a stick to prop beneath the open sash. The *objets* seemed to jump up at my fingers, like dogs. I sat on her sofa, prim, my legs crossed at the ankles, and waited a quarter of an hour until the alarm of my heart threatened to wake up the house. I took a piece of thread, the length of my hair, that I'd pulled from a pin-cushion. I couldn't tell what color it was in the dark, and when I woke the next morning in my own bed, I reached for it before I touched my glass of water.

Yellow. It was a yellow thread I'd stolen.

Saxifrageae

Saxifraga, saxifrage
S. granulata, S. tridactylites

Scalloped whorl-shaped leaves, white angel flowers, some species with red stems. (All species should have red stems; I want some too.) The old doctors, who looked only at the shapes of things—and bless them for it—saw how the roots bore funny round bulbs, pea-sized, stone-shaped, and thought, *What do those resemble but the devilish kidney stones that we old men pass from our penises in great exquisite agony, so that we might say we know something of what it's like to birth a child?* They did resemble kidney stones, so the old doctors fed saxifrage roots to their bladder-pained patients, and by god if I can find some in this climatological wasteland I'll give it a try.

I tune out Deakin, who, with his frantic clauses, knew: *We do not, however, now find that, under any circumstances, the roots of the Saxifrage* do anything but shit-little good.

"Is this midlife crisis," my brother texts.

"You're too young." I move into the shade so I can see my phone's screen, and peevishly pick through the nameless green clumps for saxifrage. If I wasn't so used to loneliness, I'd lose my f-ing mind in this Colosseum. Arch after arch after arch . . . Every few days I hear a martyr screaming.

"I want more," he writes.

Yeah, *get in line*. "We've both got holes," I write, which isn't something we've ever said before. Did he cry when she died? Did his feeling of betrayal launch him into hunger? Or did he not need a mother? I wait for him to respond, sensibly, that everyone has holes.

"I have a job," he writes. "I pay bills. You mess around. Not comparable."

I think *shit* and *don't ever let me marry a man* and *when do people learn?* "I'm hurting myself," I write. "You're hurting other people."

The red-stemmed variety is still here, check, so that's the one I dig up and chew. With little balls in my mouth is how the man with the pencil finds me again.

XVI.

Hypericineae

Hypericum perforatum, St. John's wort

Abundant yellow flowers with fine black dots; leaves all over with spots. When I sketch these in my notebook, it looks as if I've given a plant measles.

It's the warrior's balm, the *fuga daemonum*, the bane of both devils and disease. It can kill a herd of cows in a fortnight. My grandfather's field was overrun with it one summer, and the calves and their mothers greedily ate the bounty. First they grew thin, then thirsty. Some drowned in the farm pond; others lay next to their mothers and refused to nose for milk. They itched all over and rubbed against trees and fence posts and fallen rakes. Three old bulls grew so crazed they ran in rounds until they died, leaving behind perfect circles in the crop, which would not regrow for a year.

In my separate account for Deakin, I slip this in; surely a botanical student would search in a flora for tales of consequence. (Oh, I am taking to the feeling of consequence!) This journal is brown and bound—my notes for him are loose and tied with ribbon, so I will not mistake the two.

"I told you I wanted no more stories about your ancestors," he says, the ribbon wrapped around his thumb.

"Yes," I say, "but could plants serve as more than fact?"

I hear the butcher below separating the hocks from the ham. On St. John's Day, some crush *Hypericum* buds for the purple ink and mix the juice with oil to make the blood of Christ. My grandfather bought more cows; my father was well-fed; despite these graces, I still believed in theft. Which is how I met you.

XVII.

Papaveraceae

Papaver, poppy
P. rhoeas, P. dubium

If ye break faith with us who die / We shall not sleep, though poppies grow / In Flanders fields. I'm a faith-breaker; I lie to the man with the pencil when I don't tell him he has seeds in his teeth. I lie when I say yes, I *am* a botanist, and these are my notes. I flash the pages past him quick, so all he can see of my sketch is four petals, which should be shocking red except that all I have is charcoal. *Use your own blood*, I wish he'd say. But he's a man of civilization; he doesn't slip his babies whiskey to get them to sleep. (*Papaver* from "pap," from child's food, from giving them opium for quiet.)

I don't know how he's found me through the curtain of tourists, hunched as I am like a gargoyle among the stones.

I like to think it's magnetism, but maybe it's stench. The sun is casting him in halos above me. A family squeezes past us with three children on a single leash; the father glances back in disapproval. *Why isn't everyone tied to something*, he thinks. The din of competing tour guides—Japanese washing over French, over Russian—is by now no less a white noise than evening crickets.

I push my sunglasses up my nose with my middle finger, a professorial gesture. I hear him ask for a number. "Four hundred," I say. "They can make four hundred flowers a season, one plant." I think being impressive is a transitive property, and that I gain from this statistic.

He cocks his wrist—his hand has a phone in it. His mouth is either amused or not at all.

"A *number*," I say. "Ah. My number."

Four hundred, I still want to say. *Didn't you hear me? FOUR HUNDRED.*

Chelidonium majus, celandine

He floats, a ghost, above the Colosseum. It is a cure, this nipplewort, swallowwort, tetterwort. A curer of what? Warts? He looks through books and finds a forebear who clears his vision: it *consumeth away slimie things that cleave about the ball of the eye*. If he had seen the darkness coming, would he have stopped her hand?

XVIII

Capparideae

Capparis spinosa, caper tree

Why does God create the worm and the swallow? The caper shames me. In all these lowly weeds, how shocking to come upon a flower saucer-sized and pure white, stamens exploding in fuchsia and pink—as close to the Asian mimosa as our native species can attain. It is too much. Better the pickled buds—steal the flower before it opens, before it becomes too much, and douse it in salt and vinegar, let it brine. These tart pellets are closer kin to me, though let this not smell of false modesty; both of us could have been beautiful.

I have stolen flowers. I have stolen flour, and raisins, and buttermilk. The homes I first chose were the finer ones—I wanted to steal their sights. But one afternoon I left my tutor, claiming the need for air (a young-ladyish need), and walked a mile through the politeness of houses until they turned dusty and close, and when I turned into a courtyard flagged with laundry, I followed a cat as it ran up a stair, as if I daily chased this cat, my cat, the two of us twinned in play. *Brownie!* I whispered, for it was orange. *Brownie, come back!* The house was empty, dark. It smelled of cabbage. I sat on a three-legged stool while the cat ringed my ankles. A bulb of garlic hunched on the windowsill below a spider's web, and in my young mind it seemed that the spider and I were of the same species, with the same requirements.

I left the cat and the spider and took the garlic.

Imagine telling the soldier this story; imagine him grasping my fingers with new endearment, sniffing my skin for the remnant of this crime. Saying *I too* when I speak of confinement and impotence. No—I can hear you laughing an ocean away.

Capparis, a mischievous decumbent, grows straight out of walls, as if mortar is its preferred substrate, as if verticality has no ordinary relation to daily life. It reminds me of you this way, you on the boat facing nowhere, me with my skirts in the sand. I pencil a note of your beauty, so many stamens, to be read by a man with no sense of the sublime. In Ecclesiastes, there is a Hebrew word sometimes translated as *desire* and sometimes as *caper berry*—not even the ancients could distinguish. I sketch the caper leaping from a column's height, a swift, a suicide.

XIX.

Cistineae

Helianthemum guttatum, spotted rock rose

A cleistogamous plant is one that needs no pollinator; it impregnates itself, thank you. Why, then, has the rock rose dressed itself so attractively? Five yellow petals, each with a red mark at its base, the spot varying in size from pin-tiny to splotchy-big, like women with their breasts. Why look so fine if you don't need a wasp to see? Even worse, you independent lady, you barely have the strength to hang on to your clothes. Deakin calls this *fugacious*, meaning simply that your petals last three or four hours and then tremble off. A passing rodent, a breeze, the cough of a graduate student, and the irregular bosoms of the rock rose collapse—*Don't look*, they say.

I have pin-tiny breasts. My blood is marking a pad in uneven spots. I wear a blouse today with half the buttons undone—it's *hot*—knowing that it looks lovely, intending as much, and seething when a man on the street turns his head. *Seething* is too strong a word, but it evokes what I want: anger and arousal. *Bellissima*, he says. *F- you, I self-pollinate*, I respond. I'm starting to understand how too much botany might lead to revolution.

Cistus salvifolius, sage-leaved cistus

Here the white-flowered cousin to the rock rose advertises successfully, lures lusting bees with its show of good cheer, its small snackable beauty—goats flock to it when the grass has been stripped.

Deakin's note in the margin of my notes: "Fewer goats."

I crept to the house of a goat—the lawyer for my father who took me on his knee when I was young and squeezed my thighs as if they'd juice—and I sat on the dressing chair by his bed as he slept, great snores rattling his mustache, his wife cross-armed and corpse-like beside him, her hair in a cap. I thought to steal his hands. To slip the flesh off his bones and wrap them in a sack to throw in a pond. But I could not bring myself to wake him. I smelled deeply the wife's powdered cheek; I folded the sheet back from his foot so he'd grow cold; I gently spit—where, it doesn't matter.

What I finally took from that house was his razor. If his hair bushed his face in wildness, girls, I thought, might recognize a monster.

In the Colosseum there is nearly nothing so pure as the cistus, as clean as an egg, white unblemished, yellow undimmed.

XX.

Resediaceae

Reseda, rocket mignonette
R. alba, R. phytuma

The man with the pencil returns when the Colosseum closes, and I take my last few notes with furrowed brow, as if I were super smart and these plants were of immediate, nuclear-war importance.

"This one?" he asks, running a hand slowly up the inflorescence of a mignonette in a manner only botanists might consider lewd.

I tell him what long-dead Deakin said, that you give this flower to a woman if you want to say, *Your qualities surpass your charms.*

"Is that a compliment?" he asks.

I scan his clothes: an uncrisp button-up, pants that are

somewhere between regular and linen, laced brown working shoes, not Tevas, though they're rimmed in white dust. "Have you ever sent a message to a woman via flower?"

He shakes his head. He doesn't smile much for a seducer. Or maybe that's the trick; remind the ladies of their fathers.

"Well, if you ever want to tell me I'm a hideous hag but I smell nice, or talk smart, this is the one." I snap a stem off— shivering as I do it, what sacrilege—and hand it to him.

"I haven't gotten close enough to smell you," he says. I find this an appropriate response.

I scoot on my bottom to him, my head right up against his knees, and he bends and takes my hair in his hands and inhales.

XXI.

Terebinthaceae

Pistacia, turpentine-tree
P. terebinthus, P. lentiscus

From the terebinth and mastic trees we receive turpentine and gum. We crawl under the heavy red-berried branches and cut the bark in stripes until the resin bleeds. We collect the blood on stones, wait for it to dry, then scoop it into baskets at night and hide it away in the cool of a cellar. The resin is yellow or white, sweet-tasting or smoky or clear; we fill cavities with it, we mix it with oil to make paint. And the tree's flesh meanwhile is weeping, has been robbed. In the Bible they call it *bakha*, the Valley of Baca, the weeping valley, the valley of mastic.

We say the tree is there to be stripped. We say the girl is there to be plucked.

XXII.

Violaceae

Viola, violet
V. odorata, V. canina

He floats, a ghost, above the Colosseum. The sun on this stage sears all sweet violets except *there*, in the disk of shade. *There*, the purple buries itself in leaves—*don't look*—but doesn't he smell it still? He peers through scent; *par-fumer*, through smoke. He wants to set the dogs on that scent, to tame by tearing. Why didn't they let him be? He, once master, seeks vengeance on mortality.

FIG. 2

XXIII.

Fumariaceae

Fumaria, fumitory
F. capreolata, F. officinalis, F. parviflora

On stalks, two-lipped flowers—pink or white or pink-and-white, lipsticked, like dressed-up shrimp, or me at sixteen. I remember my father, wit's end, pointing to me as I stomped out the door in smudge-eyed sexual rage: "If you leave this house now, you won't leave it again!" But aren't I here, in Rome, alone?

I lived in Jackson this past summer, kicking around the old house, working part-time making milkshakes. Finishing your first year of grad school should feel like a big f-ing deal, but my dead mother did it, and look where it got her. A homemaker, a library volunteer, an amateur naturalist. No, you have to get a PhD before you're safe. I'm gunning for tenure, for Distinguished Professor, for Emerita, until there's no one left to call me a fraud. No one left to take my gun.

Last night my advisor threw a dinner party for some ex-pat academics, and I was there, and a bunch of men were there, and one woman working on microorganisms. Every-one was loud—even the woman—and when I found her in the kitchen making coffee, I asked, "Is this what you've al-ways wanted to do?"

She glanced at the French press.

"No, I mean, be a professor. When you were a kid, were you like, 'I want to be a professor.'"

She shook her head. Her hair was a big salt-and-pepper pouf. "I wanted to be an astronaut." She saw I was unsat-isfied. "I just did whatever felt like a grown-up step at the time—college, grad school."

"Financing for a car."

"*Marriage.* Like I was hoping to prove I deserved the space I took up. Prove to who? My mom? Jesus? But at some point I realized I was happy."

"In your manufactured life."

She pressed the plunger down, and the coffee moved in brown tides. "Well, *I* made it. As it turns out. Despite spend-ing half my time feeling powerless." She poured two cups. "Who's your advisor?"

I told her.

"Yeah, you have to get past that," she said.

Meaning what? Get *over* it? Push past *him?* Move on? Destroy? All I said was, pointing to the mugs, "You want me to take those out?"

"Oh," she said, "they're both for me."

Fumitories pucker for a touch. Holding their mouths open as if grace could be slipped inside, forgiveness sucked and swallowed, a tongue the best touch of all. The first time I sat in a strange man's lap, he squeezed me round the middle while my mother watched, laughing nervously, she and I both. I felt his fingers through my shirt, five nubby touches feeling at my ribs.

Polygaleae

Polygala monspeliaca, yellow-flowered milkwort

I had an old uncle who grew milkwort for his cows, some perhaps inherited from my grandfather's herd, who was convinced the papery veined flowers turned to milk in his herd's udders, and sold his milk at market at a discount, given how much more he produced (he believed) than his neighbors. I doubt his science was ever proven, but this is how I would like to move through life. Calling it bounty and giving it away.

My father took me to a concert yesterday evening against my protests (I had sketches to perfect) and sat me down, with mock surprise, next to the soldier. The men shook out their coattails like proud ducks. The music was Monteverdi, ancient, and I sat between my father and the man he wanted for my husband and counted the pleats in my skirt.

At intermission, the young man brought me champagne in a shallow glass the shape of a lotus flower. "Your face is turning brown," he said. "You might consider a larger hat."

"Does the nation not need laborers?" I asked.

"Yes, but also women."

I smiled and tied my two silk gloves into a knot. I tried to summon what you might say, your loudness like a trumpet of Gabriel, but you weren't there. "I believe you'd find there's much to learn from nature that cannot be perceived when fully swaddled." If you could have heard me, only a month in the field and declaring myself a botanist! The grand performance of women, perhaps: turning what little we are given into how much we can make.

"I have no objections to a learned lady, but isn't that the purpose of books? Just as one might cherish a clean home but employ a housemaid to create the effect."

"You prefer the veneer."

"I prefer," he said, taking the hand of mine that wasn't twisting fabric, "beauty—in any form."

I stepped away from him, dear. I did not say, *I have more than I need; I will give you the surplus for free.*

XXV.

Leguminosae

Spartium junceum, Spanish broom

I am Spartium! A giant shrub, as spiky gold as Southern forsythia, but here in Italy they made their houses of it, before the era when houses were meant to be sturdy.

The man with the pencil took me last night to a bar, or whatever the Romans call it: drinks, darkness, dancing.

The broom's stems hold all its water, so the leaves can fall off at will. The stems are what's harvested to sweep; the leaves no one remembers.

He didn't ask me about my work, which I thought was admirable until I didn't. What did he think I was, just a hot set of limbs? We talked too much about politics.

"What's the worst thing you've ever done to a woman?" I asked.

Deakin adored the shepherds in the broom huts. He described them more minutely than the plants, right down to the men's furry goatskin coats, which made them most *patriarchal-looking*. How funny a storyteller he was, how tuned in to weird gender shit.

The man ran his hand along his jawline, scratching the stubble there. Took a sip. Narrowed his eyes as he stared at the rows of liquor modeling in front of the mirror, him dredging through depths, perhaps unaware that the bottles in their shapeliness looked like girls posing. Consumable. I found a clock on the wall so I could track the time that was passing. *This*, I wanted to say. *This is the worst thing you've done to a woman.*

Cytisus laburnum, laburnum-tree

Called golden rain, a black-wooded tree that spills long racemes of slipper-shaped flowers. Poison to horses; treat to hares. Humans have tried it both ways, with no resolution.

I never took what I thought would get me caught, but I couldn't always determine what was valuable in a human's home: what was trash, what was gift. I stole a letter from a child's nightstand, the sleeping girl too young to read or write, and only in the morning when I examined my prey did I find the note from a mother: *If I should not return, be good for Cousin Paolo, and hug Beppe, pretending it's me.*

My right hand shook all day.

I lurked the next night to evaluate this Paolo, to gauge whether I should steal the girl-child instead, rescue her from horror, but he was old and blind and there was a housekeeper with a solid gut living in the attic who looked by the set of her sleeping brow that she would stand for no cheek, not from no man, so I left the letter where I found it and forgave the mother, who was certainly no worse than I. It comforted me, in fact, to think some stranger might once have been at *my* bedside, that someone had read *my* secrets and had let me live.

Anthyllis vulneraria, kidney vetch

Also known as lady's finger, not from its delicacy or the fingeriness of its pods, but because its gauzy coating was once used to stanch open wounds—like, I guess, by girl nurses. Flowers in balls, leaves imparipinnate, a word that is woefully underused. It just means the leaves go marching two by two along a stem, even-steven, until the end, when the whole cluster is topped by a single leaf, a pairless leaf, a leaf mortally alone. (See, my bristle-faced advisor, I *have* been at my books.)

Sometimes I imagine I run into my advisor at one of those bars—drinks, darkness, dancing—and he has a woman looped in his arm, and the woman looks like me but is fifty. In the dream future, I have given up and loved him. That's where all bad stories are headed anyway.

In the present, he looks at my week's bundle of notes and says my handwriting brings shame upon the discipline and there's no way I saw a kidney vetch because it hasn't grown in the Colosseum in a hundred and fifty years.

"Then it's about time," I say. I don't know how we got so adversarial. Every time I speak I worry he'll read my impertinence as a female emotion.

In truth, I marked the vetch on an afternoon when the man with the pencil was visiting and I wanted to look impressively occupied, which really throws the whole science of observation into question, and maybe this is what I'll propose for my thesis, the abstract of which is due in December—a comparative study of how scientists' hearts affect their vision. My guess: lovers see the least of all.

Ononis, rest-harrow
O. spinosa, O. arvensis

In Russia they dipped their swords in extract of rest-harrow, then went riding angry-faced into the wind to cure the steel. But these peas remind me more of nuns' cornettes, or the white hats of Brittany, a pink pointed face buried in a cowl. I think again of Sister Benedetta, and Sister Bartolomea, and the way their bodies must have called Christ to mind.

Could we not have done that?

Could we not have nunned?

Melilotus, melilot
M. italica, M. indica

Hot damn, I found *indica*. I star it in my notes; I garland myself with it. It used to be called *Ghirlanda*, garland-flower, for how they'd swing it around the necks of conquering heroes, and now I'm wondering about the painter Ghirlandaio and if he was some special stud of a victor. (No—he was only victor, in history's long and fickle game, over his father, the original Ghirlandaio, who made small crowns out of metal to decorate the Florentine ladies' hairdos.) I once saw a portrait of his in Lisbon; it was of a garlandless lady whose look of mingled apprehension and resignation seemed so wearily familiar to me. She was prettier than I am—most portraits are—but had we shared a century we would've known something true about each other. She saw the shit. She was a shit-seer, and thank god there was a man with a brush to mark it down.

When I show my advisor the crushed leaf, with its distinctive smell of coumarin (the compound released when your grass is cut), he says, "This looks more like *Ononis*," so I take the leaf and shove it in my mouth.

With great patience he watches me chew. "Did you know they add melilot to Gruyère?" he says. "That's where the cheese gets its taste."

"Mm," I say, my mouth feeling bitter and dry. I thought

grad school would be nerds nerding out together, not sadists taking advantage of masochists.

"So if it's indeed melilot, you must be tasting Gruyère. Are you?" His eyes are blue and sharp. It feels like we're speaking at half speed, like one of us is holding a detonator. I want to ask, just in case, whether *Ononis* is poisonous.

There's nothing else I can say. "Yes."

He leans back in his chair, the battle over. "*Melilotus*," he says.

"Delicious," I say. I swallow.

Trifolium, trefoil
T. pratensis, T. ochroleucum, T. stellatum,
T. scabrum, T. arvensis, T. repens, T. nigresecus,
T. hybridum, T. procumbens, T. filiforme, T. tomentosum,
T. resupinatum, T. subterraneum

As a six-year-old girl, I wished on a clover that my mother would die, and she didn't.

Lotus, bird's-foot trefoil
L. corniculatus, L. ornithopodiodes

These trefoils resemble rabbits in a row—four or three or five orange bunnies with noses trembling, circling a single stalk. I wish I'd been some better man's assistant (*cough,*

Linnaeus) so I could've had a hand in naming. Cripes, the power! *Lotus cuniculus, cuniculauribus.* Rabbit ears.

This is how I would name the man with the pencil: born of leisure, of a man and a woman who long before they met had decided to perpetuate a civilized dream. Raised in the conviction that to *dream* meant to *aspire*, and so swimming in a marijuana haze while the Stones spun round was discouraged—not by word, but by facial tic. The child became old-fashioned. Educated in the liberal tradition, in which all the change meant to occur had already done so, so what remained was conservatism. The boys wore the same brown shoes, turned up their nose at Frosted Flakes. Went to college and encountered girls, and boys who liked boys, and girls who were maybe boys, and those who liked no one at all. But love wasn't what life was about. The books in hardback, in leather sets, were of history and battle and thought. His excuse when he broke girls' hearts: he was too consumed by the weight of the world to continue in such pleasure. *Such pleasure*, the girls would repeat hopefully. *What weight?* said one. Found a posting abroad, a tech company or a banking firm or a pharmaceutical bloodsucker, some way of making money that seemed, because so little labor had to be expended, polite on the verge of criminal. Decades ago when his father played Tchaikovsky in the nursery, he'd absorbed the lesson his parents didn't even know was at the heart of their civilized dream: taste is not made, but copied. And so on a Monday afternoon he took in the great round of the Colosseum. The first Monday of the month, because the day before had been free to the masses, and not only was he willing to pay, he wanted to pay on the day when the sunburned families with their unending crackling maps would be least likely to intrude. The sight of a woman in a dress in the dirt would have signaled *submission* to him, and *vulnerability*, and maybe *Pre-Raphaelite*, depending on how wild her (my) hair was. Easy to drop a pencil. Easier still to hold her head in your hands. Easiest of all to listen, and wait, and abstain.

Homo ignavus.

When I look at him I start to think about my thesis, and I get aroused.

Trigonella corniculata, horse-shoe fenugreek

Without the strident scent of its cousin, *T. foenum-graecum*, but with the same saw-edged leaves and small yellow seeds, the ingestion of which will cause one's breast milk to smell of maple. If one's breasts produce milk. If one has a baby and a dish of fenugreek seeds, both.

I found another child when I was sixteen, just a mite in a crib, that I considered thieving. My fingers parted its tiny tuber toes, which curled like a sundew catching a fly. It was the butcher's house, and I was there for his knives—or one knife, or anything sharp. (I didn't yet know who would come to live above.) I had a thought that I could steal his killing power, and that in missing some totem he would collapse. The flanks would run free. But instead he had a little living thing, far sharper than what I came for.

I had not been touched by a man. You've never believed me, so many have been your wounds, but I say it again. In the dark with the thing's white fat lit by the moon, a fantasy surged in me, greater than any dream of being broken into (and as a girl I did have those): a dream of being broken *out* of. A great rupturing, multiplying, a gauntlet thrown in flesh.

I leaned down to brush my nose against its fair hair. It began to squall, and the reverie ended. I stripped its swaddling cloth away and left the thing screaming and naked. At home I wrapped the cloth around my neck and pressed my breasts one and then the other, back and forth, pressing and pressing, until I fell asleep.

Medicago, medick
M. lupulina, M. orbicularis, M. minima, M. maculata, M. denticulata, M. terebellum, M. tribuloides

Usually I'm not into babies, but *Medicago*'s seedpods are wacky as a dream: the giant translucent discs of *orbicularis*, the crowding pill bugs of *lupulina*, the horny burred Babel of *denticulata*.

And medick's fed on not by men, but by more dreams. Moths. The turnip moth, common swift, flame. Nutmeg, lime-speck pug, latticed heath. The setaceous Hebrew character.

Imagine being ravished by a setaceous Hebrew character and then birthing a snail-shaped burr. High romance, friends. (I've been ravished without romance, without powdered wings, and left with no seed at all.) But the "character" on the back of that moth happens to be *nun*. So maybe there is no love but in isolation. *Not isolation*, the blasted monastics would say, *but orthodoxy*.

Shall I find a moth and catechize him into love?

I send a picture to my brother, ask about the home front. I'm feeling manic today, hungry for more. On windless days the heat seeps into my ears like far-off voices. If you press your cheek to the shell of the Colosseum, you'll hear death rattles. My brother says he suggested counseling (good!), and his wife said okay in that sweet wife way, and they worked up the courage, put on smart clothes, and *bam*: first session, she confesses. Had an affair while pregnant.

"Say WHAT," I text.

"Only kissing."

I laugh aloud from the second tier of seats, and the weeds above me toss in the sound. I can see it all: her jewellike pink tears, his flabbergastery, the counselor's panic, and then her muffled postscript, the final damnation: *We kissed two times.*

I like reading about the wild convents of centuries past, where nuns snuck through tunnels to consort with monks or slipped into a sister's cell for some PG-13 cuddling, and I would want my brother's wife's innocence there, her expertly sharpened sense of guilt. Maybe there is no love but in failure.

"What now," I text.

Long pause. It's early morning in Mississippi; the baby must be fending off the day's first mosquitoes. His wife's still asleep, eyes puffy. He has to get to work soon, but all his exits have turned to swamps. I stare at my phone until I realize he's not writing back.

Vicia, vetch
V. onobrychoides, V. cracca, V. gracilis, V. uniflora, V. sativa, V. anguistifolia, V. lutea, V. hybrida

The soldier had me to dinner last night—had my father, rather; asked for my accompaniment, as one would ask for a raincoat or a cane—and said I ate like I'd been starved. My father's exasperated brows. "She's sturdy," he explained. "No consumptive," though he knew a wisp is prettier than a presence.

I was always hungry, without cause; my parents had paunches, our house had maids. (Long live the Republic.) The pantry was my hideout, and I took communion there before I found farther sanctuaries. Putting grapes or biscuits or almonds in my mouth meant adding to myself. I am me plus this.

Vetch was among the earliest domesticated crops. Neolithic women used to sow it in the ground, sit on stools to watch it sprout, tend it, water it, weed it, beat the men away from it, admire the purple pea flowers, wind the flowers in their coarse Neolithic hair, praise one another with words like *Love, you look as sweet as vetch today*, and one day in autumn pick the beans to boil and eat.

And then it became a "crop of last resort"; we don't eat it anymore.

I ate the entire wing of chicken placed on my plate. I sucked the bones clean, quietly. When the soldier asked if my father had kept me locked in the attic all week, he answered, "God willing, one day you too might raise a daughter," and I answered, "And throw away the key."

Vetch is fed to cows, who are never asked not to eat.

Lathyrus, vetchling
L. aphaca, L. sativa, L. pratensis, L. sylvestris

I'm not a kid of farmers. I don't tend to put things in my mouth that don't come from fluorescently lit stores. (Though there was a tomato plant once, a balcony monster, whose fruit I plucked and fed to friends. I hate tomatoes; I planted it because some guy said it was easy to grow, and *grow* sounded like a word that could save.) So I have fairly limitless admiration for ancient peoples who experimented with putting random f-ing plants in their mouths. The grass pea, for instance, sporadically causes paralysis and emaciation of the butt. Those who should not eat the grass pea: most humans, cows, swine, horses, chickens, and pigeons. Those who can: *some* humans, certain Swiss cattle, all sheep. Poor people used

to make bread out of *Lathyrus* flour, and their legs and arms
went stiff until they tweaked the ratio of vetch to wheat in the
flour, and then I guess they thawed, or else they let the frozen people die and tried again with the next batch. Is bread
that irresistible? The Grand Duke of Württemberg forbade
grass pea flour altogether in 1671. I like to picture him, Württemberg, fat and bewigged, the white from his powder falling
on his shoulders, his quill in his mouth, staining his wooden
teeth: "What *shall* we do about the plague of rigid limbs?"
No one else is in the room but a maid who's been sworn not to
speak. Her own mother is lying in bed at home with a left arm
stuck out, permanently right-angled. "I should not eat vetch,
sire," she whispers. He rewards her that night by taking her
into his ocean of a bed, where she goes still and silent and
thinks of the swine tipped over in their pens, the swine who
cannot move, and the sheep who can.

My advisor brings a friend to the Colosseum; they tour
the ruin while I crouch along its perimeter, sunscreen sweating into my eyes. The place has good acoustics.

"What's she working toward?" the friend says in water-
proof cargo pants. "Her thesis is taxonomical?"

"Her thesis? I doubt she'll produce one."

"Just an assistant?"

"The Tenzing to my Hillary," my advisor laughs.

"Surely we think of Tenzing Norgay now as a mountain-
eer," says the friend.

I scoot out of range, draw violent peaks on my notes,

swear to buy cargo pants of my own, right after I defend my f-ing dissertation.

Scorpiurus subvillosa, four-flowered caterpillar

The seedpods curl back in spines, presenting a sort of scorpion's tail.

Deakin, having developed some trust in these few weeks, offers to train me in the work of description in addition to taxonomy. He's at his desk above the butcher's, from whom I nearly nabbed an infant, his wall of plant texts ripe with blood-smell. His sleeves rolled up to his white puckered elbows. He is the father no one would wish for their child. (You told me finding a baby would be my own business.)

"If you compare a *Scorpiurus* to a scorpion, aren't you merely making an echo?" he says. "Do you have no original observations?"

"Then," I say, "it looks like an emotion. Like the curling pain of my heart when my lover left."

He laughs, that man, until he farts. My womanhood here is a great joke.

Coronilla varia, purple coronilla

Take a cute flower and ring a dozen round a radius, and thus easily life is improved. The man with the pencil asked me out again. (Yes, I know: *Don't date a jackass.*) In some error

I passed him my correct number, not the old U.S. time-and-date hotline, which used to also provide weather details.

"Sorry about our last encounter," he says, which I try to remember. This time we meet at a café on a hill overlooking the Colosseum's ticket line. We drink tiny civilized coffees. "I was feeling distracted."

"It's not news if a man doesn't pay attention to me." I'm making origami out of my three empty sugar packets. The heels of my hands are dry and calloused, rubbed red from pawing at the Colosseum's stones.

"Can I get a chance at redemption?"

His hair is so thick I can't see the light through it. Mine feels limp, a thin ponytail for yanking around. His foot beneath the table keeps accidentally, or maybe not, banging against mine.

"I'm asking," he says, leaning forward, "because I like a long game."

"You're here for six months before your firm sends you to the next project. You're bored and horny."

"You're bored and horny."

"No, I'm pursuing a fascinating career and am also horny."

"You can't imagine at all why I might be interested, beyond a hookup?"

I don't like the way his eyes always smile, like he's some hypnotic Nostradamus. He rubs the handle of his tiny cup provocatively. It's confidence. I have never once felt what he is feeling in this moment, despite having scraped and scrabbled and bit to get here. To this job, this age, alive.

"You like me," I say. He is also, maybe, innocent.

He takes my hand, puts my torn fingernails to his soft mouth.

Ornithopus scorpioides, purslane-leaved bird's-foot

"It resembles a bird and a scorpion in battle," I tell Deakin.

"Now you tease."

I do. It looks, in fact, like a great smooth whale. Leaves in sets of three, one large and glaucous, ovate, plunging forward into air like a whale's beak, and the other two small and sessile, clinging to the stem like fins, propelling the beast with grace, with timidity. A plant covered with whales, each nosing into the light.

I take the pencil from Deakin's desk as I leave, simply waft it into my hand as my skirts float by, a mere ballooning woman making breezes, absorbing property. There is no thrill except in the story: in bed tonight I can close my eyes and see it unfold. An idea strikes him, he fumbles for the pencil, finds only empty space, bends over beneath the desk to look among the lost leaves and crumbs—nothing—turns to the window, thinking perhaps a raven has flown in and out again, but the window is closed, only a notch in the pane where months before a hawk made an attempt on his life. This is Deakin's illusion, that he is under siege, a story to which I happily contribute. What puts me to sleep at last is the certainty that after all this, for want of a pencil the idea's been lost.

Securigera coronilla, hatchet-vetch

He brings a wedge of cheese to the Tiber. We meet on the bridge, and I've done my hair so it looks thick but not Pre-Raphaelite, added lipstick as an insurance against getting kissed. I eat all the cheese, not realizing it was a snack to share. I question my own needs: Is it him I want, or food? Not him; yes, food but also yes, a generalized wish for company of the dangerous kind. I don't understand why we don't arm ourselves for dates as we do for war. What's a negotiation without a weapon?

I picture my sister-in-law in counseling, hatchet raised, defending her right to embrace a man who doesn't move like a glacier when she asks for diaper help. She knows now she should've had the hatchet on their first night out, back when my brother opened car doors and called her angel. It's a family failure, I admit; we didn't raise him right. We were lost in separate rooms, not thinking any of us would ever love again.

The man with the pencil brushes his hand along my bare leg, and my fear and gratitude commingle.

Umbelliferae

Sanicula europaea, wood-sanicle

The Germans say of two species, "He who has sanicle and self-heal needs neither physician nor surgeon." But sanicle is a shadow plant—carrying its blooms in balls on stalks, like candies on sticks—and hides in the hypogeum, far from *Prunella vulgaris*, the necessary self-heal.

In these dark spots of the Colosseum I listen more intently to the prickles on my skin. Here on the floor was once a cemetery, the old battleground backfilled with bodies after the emperors had gone. And where are the graves? A farmer passes by, dragging his goat by a rope. An old woman gums a song, nowhere near. I ally myself with the ancient nymphs, those women at work who were waylaid by gods disguised as beasts. A crow dips by, and I crouch. When a whip snake slides against my heel and asks who I'm mourning, I tell the story of a woman I met in her bed at night twelve months ago, and met again at a funeral, and again in her bed, the daughter of a banker who was promised to a count, who taught me how a woman's body is born and how it's broken.

Where is the self-heal? In the sun?

Eryngium campestris, field-eryngo

He floats, a ghost, above the Colosseum. The girl creeps closer to thistly pain, to Satan's mace. He breathes a breeze on the back of her neck. Taste it, he sighs; the only way down is to sugar it, so sugar it and swallow. Wrench-and-yum *Eryngium*. There'll be stigmata on the stomach where the bloom goes down—blood on the bush where the blossom is lost. He sees every streak of red the Colosseum held, and it's all red.

Aegopodium podagraria, gout-weed

The monks were fond of this triangular-stemmed species, maybe because it's so f-ing hardy it can resprout from a discarded inch of rhizome. We don't usually compare monks and cockroaches, but there's a similar insistence on survivalism; give me privation, punish me with chastity, hurl me into the wilderness, and I'll keep on reproducing these obnoxious green shoots of faith. No one wants *Aegopodium* in their gardens, just like no one wants Jesus. We're justifiably wary of That Which Cannot Be Killed.

One night, late teens, I had a dream my mother was alive—how original—and she grabbed my forearms and squeezed them hard and I thought, *Yes, hurt me*, and I stared at the bruising flesh rather than her face, stared at her nails, that clutch, those broken veins, purple, the wash of blood beneath skin, because her face would've been too much. I call her dead so I won't ever again wake up having forgotten.

I still hear her voice, though here I hear others. Ghosts in my ear, men, shrill. Always wanting not to die. We ladies, we've gotten over it, made death a tool.

I'm feeling so buffeted by wanting more and settling for less that not until my head's on the pillow do I realize I gave my advisor the wrong set of weekly notes. Not the notes with location details and soil conditions for the Umbelliferae, but the notes with violent doodles and thesis ideas and sketches of what I think the man with the pencil's dick looks like and also *F- HILLARY*, which is a reference to Edmund Hillary but which could certainly be interpreted differently in this era of American politics, and my eyes shoot open and I think *shit shit shit shit shit.*

Bupleurum, hare's-ear
B. aristatum, B. odontites, B. rotundifolia

He floats, a ghost, above the Colosseum. Here in his notes—her notes?—he learns it's called thorough-wax, that is, thorough-growing (as the moon grows when it waxes, the moon above this empty bowl), stems through leaves in per-foliate punctures. What needs interrupting more than a leaf? A woman. Shh, a woman.

Oenanthe peucedanifolia, water dropwort

The involucre—the nest of bracts, half-leaf, half-petal—is wanting. You once asked me what I wanted for, what I lacked. Why I snuck through darkness to take what wasn't mine, vomiting in the morning at my own shame. (No; I told you I vomited. Most mornings I merely blushed on my pillow, snuck my hand under the sheet to find the thread or book or spoon, and rubbed it until I shone.) Does one need lack to register gain?

I can hold my hands so ultimately still that I sometimes think I have died. That is my thieving secret. The window peels open soundlessly. I pass my palms over a sleeping body, not a tremor. I have taken a necklace off a napping bosom. (I put it on her vanity.) Once I lifted a cat and something about my cold immobility convinced it I was still the marble floor, and it stretched out, undisturbed. I am undisturbing.

Foeniculum vulgare, common fennel

There's no getting the journal back. What am I going to do, break into his office? I head back to the Colosseum, keep working, wait for punishment. What makes me most anxious is not the dick doodles but my seedling ideas for the thesis, which I think are really good but which are tiny and new and if he shits all over them—

I want to do everything my advisor's *not* doing—i.e., *caring* about something. What if you had this exact same project, documenting species like a snapshot of life—this is what is— but you added humanity and meaning? (Here's where I get kicked out of STEM.) Maybe that's only possible where I'm from, where people snack on stories all day long, which is what reminds me that Jackson has a Coliseum too: weedy, I always thought, but hell, now I know everything's a weed. Thanks, advisor, wherever you are, ears steaming like a cartoon.

I root more wildly around the edges of the amphitheater. F- him. F- fennel. I'm an unabashed admirer of most Roman food, from hot balls of fried rice to the pungent artichoke, but there is one vegetable I can't abide—raw, stewed, boiled, baked, roasted, fried, in a soup, or in a salad—and that's f-ing *Foeniculum*. Look how innocently it grows: feathery, fairy, like dill, great yellow umbels.

A tourist spies me hunched over the specimen and raises his camera. I lower my head so my eyes appear above my sunglasses. He pauses. My eyes narrow. He shifts his lens to the left, toward a heap of blond stone. *Yes*, I think, *when your children see that snapshot in the family album, tell them you meant to aim at a woman crouched around a shrub.* With my fingers petting the needle-thin fennel leaves, I follow his shuffling until he rejoins a woman, her skirt so long she must be a wife, and they don't touch or look at each other but move forward together, like two impersonal streams forming a river, headed to the same trattoria, the same hotel, the same flight home, the same sagging mattress on a street named after a tree somewhere in suburban Ohio, a tree that hasn't been seen to grow in that area for years.

Ferula communis, giant fennel

The day after I stole a ring—silver, with a small opal clasped in the center by a claw—I accompanied my mother to church, and as she proceeded down the aisle in her loud black skirts I stopped. The ring was in my bodice, feeling like a flame. I could not follow her. God was sitting at the altar, and His golden unrolling presence stopped at the edge of the nave. The few feet between that holy reach and the door to the street was where I stood, transfixed. Not ashamed, but frozen. This space with its own small font was built for penitents, those too riddled with sin to sit with the flock. My mother looked back at me accusingly, made her genuflection, deflated into the pew. I couldn't advance with the ring in my chest. But I wasn't a penitent. I have rarely been affected by

FIG. 3

God in my life, but this was a time when I felt His hand held out: *This place is not thine.* I stood for the entire mass in this limbo of the church called the narthex.

In ancient times, the giant fennel was named narthex. Also scourge. Those who whip themselves know the meaning.

Daucus muricatus, prickly-seeded carrot

Queen Anne's lace, *Daucus carota*, has been spotted in basically every iteration of the *Flora Colisea* except 1855, which suggests to me either that Deakin was drunk, his assistant was daft, or some moony boy-child snuck in at midnight and dug up all the wild carrots—the roots for his hungry ma, the giant white umbels for his sweetheart, who would of course have been allergic—leaving an inexplicable *D. carota* blank in the mid-nineteenth-century record. *Funny*, Deakin might've thought, *I have them in my own garden.* This is the central fallacy of botanical endeavors. That what is familiar ought to be familiar, and what is strange ought to be strange.

Instead, he just found *D. muricatus*, which isn't a bad carrot; in fact its bundle of purple-spiked fruit, gathered up like a goth bouquet, makes it unusually appealing, but the gaps haunt the process. What didn't he find because _____? What am I not finding because I too am _____?

I stretch my neck back to scan the highest remaining ring of the Colosseum's round walls. I almost expect to see a stone pine bursting out of the rock, eighty feet tall.

My father, who hasn't spoken much in the past decade, put his hand on my shoulder the night before I hopped the plane to Rome and said, quiet, "Don't forget us." I wanted to say I *need* to. Looking for these plants homesick is like reading a book distracted; I keep landing on the same sentence. *Daucus muricatus.* There. *Daucus muricatus.* I check my phone; no messages. How can I forget? *Daucus muricatus.* Let me move on.

Caucalis daucoides, small bur parsley

It was your ring. Yours that burned a hole in the linen closest to my breast. Its golden claw like the green hooked spines of the *Caucalis* fruit. (I only see spines in retrospect.)

The house was set back from the street, a courtyard behind a wall separating the movement from the still. No one passed through the wooden doors, tall as Polyphemus, but merchants and suitors and you and your kin. And after midnight, me. The hot scent of some rose drew me, my hand pushing at the soft wood, the hinges quieted with the olive oil I carried in a flask. That terrace was almost too much: draping shapes of plumbago and vine, shrubs in pots leaking perfume, a wilderness swallowing the stones smoothed down by generations of shoes. I didn't know anything about plants then, only what my mother grew. Not what could grow, or why.

I climbed a tree into your room because I was small, not

knowing it was yours, only that the tree would hold me. I could say I saw your face first, that even in sleep it sang at me, that I could mark the beginning of time with the sight of your hair splayed like a delta on the pillow, but no—it was the opal. I was after fire, and yours was hidden in sleep.

Torilis, hedge parsley
T. infesta, *T. nodosa*

Also known as tall sock–destroyer and short sock–destroyer. What's the difference, the height of the plant or the height of the sock? And doesn't the genus predate the invention of socks? What did they call *Torilis* in the Middle Ages? Stocking-bane?

It doesn't matter, my advisor would say. They're gone.

What does it take to survive in this world, as a woman, as a weed?

The temperatures are rising. I look for the missing parsleys in the shade, wondering if their last resort is to creep into the cool. Surely that's how evolution works: a plant picks itself up and crawls to a more hospitable patch of dirt.

But that's not how women work, I can hear my advisor say.

I haven't heard from him yet; I'm still waiting to be damned. I dream about him in a bathrobe, saying *women women* low into a microphone, and I wake up in a stain of sweat.

Scandix pecten-veneris, shepherd's needle

He floats, a ghost, above the Colosseum. He spies the wicked plant—see the *x*, the *p*, the *v*—fruits erect as soldiers, thin as ladies, green as gills. He taunts the girl to find it. The needles belong to the beggar, the clock, the crow; Adam, the Devil, Puck; the witch, the shepherd—bad woman, good man. Called Venus's comb, Mary's comb—whore, whore. He claws at his own green gills. Who killed him but a whore.

Chaerophyllum temulentum, rough chervil

One of the earliest Umbelliferae to flower, a child in the April fields. If given to humans, this particular chervil produces symptoms of severe drunkenness (*temulentus*, "tipsy"): staggering, nausea, dizziness. The heart will eventually stop, if given to humans.

There's a strange innocence in this passive voice, *if given to*. Who is it that gives, but women?

Smyrnium olusatrum, common alexanders

One of the common alexanders was Alex Rayburn, age fifteen, who wore a ladies' scarf (slinky, red-flowered) to the cross-country team's pool party the August before my sophomore year. There are alexanders who can pull that off, whose masculinity is so far beyond the bounds of doubt that rules fall like cut grass. It was the red flowers I saw, my eyes bound, rather than his body. It was the silk I felt, scrabbling, rather than skin.

Deakin's words: *stout*; *erect*; *greatly dilated*; *membranous*; *cut*; *crowded*; *nearly black*.

I thank god it's gone. I don't care that *Smyrnium* was nitrophilous, temperate, humid-loving, and that Rome now is baked and barren. There are sacrifices I would make again and again, alexanders I would slay until extinct.

XXVII.

Rhamneae

Rhamnus alternatus, broad alternate-leaved buckthorn

Was there a buckthorn in your garden? Was it February, was it flowering, were you sleeping under wool? Or did I see your shoulder exposed, and it was June, and the ten-foot shrub was dropping its red-black fruit on the white court-yard stones? Did I hear bees nuzzling for its honey?

The ring fit my finger. (Was the gold cool to the touch? Was it spring?) I only looked at you to measure my guilt. I was a thief not of value, but of meaning. And perhaps I would've put it back if you had been an old woman with a sad lined face, or a man with a roll of fat around his neck. Perhaps I didn't know it had meaning until I saw its owner. But then there was nothing I could do. I needed there to be no distinction between us. If you had awakened and proclaimed your ownership with angry, sleep-glazed eyes? But you didn't. You were too warm, wrapped in wool, or you were too warm, a summer breeze on your cheeks.

Paliurus aculeatus, Christ's thorn

I don't believe in Jesus as a savior, but I believe in him as a man who was forced into a relationship with plants. The weirdest thing about the shrub that offered its branches to be wrapped around Christ's head is that its thorns come in pairs: one straight, one reflexed. One true and one kinky. One good, one evil. Is there a way the length of *Paliurus* could've been twisted around so its straight thorns lay flat against the Messiah's head? Or is it by design impossible to avoid impalement? Did God—fine, let's assume Him—craft the *Paliurus* millennia ago knowing He would have a future Son who'd need tormenting of the cruelest kind? And did He imbue that plant with symbolism so that later believers would look at its paired thorns and see the choices laid before them in their own lives? Either I shall be righteous, or I shall be swerved?

My advisor sends me an email, says he needs to return something of mine.

Of course Christ's thorn too has vanished from the Colosseum.

XXVIII.

Araliaeae

Hedera helix, common ivy

There's nothing so common as ivy. Invasive, undying, even if hacked back to the stub.

Love too has tiny rootlets that search out trunks and stone and brick. Love too can topple a tree too small to hold it. Love too makes a hidden home for mice. It grows roots along its stems that make contact, adhere, pull closer, tighten into a lock.

I hold back my bound journal when I give my week's notes to Deakin, who smells the loose pages before he reads them—searching I think for veracity, as if I hid myself in a ladies' powder room to imagine my way into the dust and green of the Colosseum—and below my notes on umbels and ovate leaves, he writes his poem. *The former splendour and greatness of Rome's temples, baths, towers, palaces, and tombs, / Over which the Ivy now throws her slender arms and ever-shadowing mantle.* Ivy to him isn't love but a woman. Love is a woman, one-sided. Rome is a woman, conquered, embraced, brought low. A poem is a woman, rhymed and put away. He hands back the sheaf of notes and puts a question in his eyes: *Have I not done more than you?* Yes, I say with a servant's smile. You who cannot love are Master.

XXIX.

Onograriae

Circaea lutetiana, enchanter's nightshade

Did you know the Romans called Paris *Lutetia*, "Witch City"? As burns go, I'd call that simple, classic, and to the point. From the city of sorceresses comes this nightshade, airy and light and funnily not all that poisonous. But downy-stalked and downy-fruited, like a lady at Montmartre who hasn't shaved. It sneaks in the darkest cracks, and thus has earned a reputation for general nastiness. *Circaea* from Circe, that bad girl. Alas, I need something more deadly to clear the field of foes.

My eye flits ahead to the next species on the list, willow-herb, which the Jackson icon Welty knew because it was also called fireweed and was the first thing growing in the craters left by 1940s bombs, their seeds lying dormant for however-many years until a blast set them sprouting. *Is it true*, Eudora asked the man she loved who didn't love her back, who was in Rome, where people go who cannot love. *I sort of hope the turmoil did not touch them that way though.*

I sort of hope the willowherb lives on still, but I'm scared to look. I wonder if Welty ever reached for more, or if Welty was a badass witch, or both.

Epilobium, willow-herb
E. hirsutum, E. montanum

I reach to touch. Four-petaled pink flowers, notched, like a fairy cross, or a splay of vulvas. Through hairy stems comes a secretion that smells like apples and cream.

Out in the bright world you tried to coax words from my shy throat. You were training me, I think, to live without you. On one walk you bought carnation stems from a ragged woman, who kept a reluctant grip on them. "It's men should be paying," she said.

"Ah, and what do we think of that?" you said, turning to me.

My color rose. I wanted to say the thing that would please you, that would please myself. "Men *should* pay," I tried with a glint, and the woman laughed and spit and released the blooms. White, for pure love, not carnal.

We were wicked that night and drew blood and put our drops in the flowers' vase, and by morning the white had turned red.

XXX.

Valerianeae

Centranthus ruber, red valerian

Kiss-me-quick! My dead mother tried to plant this every year, its fuchsia flowers dangling over the daisies and dianthus for a few weeks before Mississippi scorched it into dust. I don't know where she got the idea: some travel in England, maybe. She loved trying to identify the brushstroke blooms in art. It was futile, I tried to tell her; the painters were just making blobs. In the few days when the valerian was still noble-headed, she'd grab me when I passed it and smother me with kisses while I screamed and swore I'd never walk by it again, inside feeling red with love.

I told this story to one man, who then tried it every time we saw a flower even vaguely magenta, until I had to tell him it wasn't valerian, and his kisses weren't the ones I wanted. I wish I'd said this earlier, to all my exes.

To the man with the pencil, I try saying nothing at all about plants. To my advisor—

"I didn't read through this," he says, gesturing to the field journal on his desk, open to the *F- HILLARY* page.

"Really sorry about that," I say. "A mix-up."

"And I don't want to give you a lecture on professionalism."

"Did you happen to read the part about the Jackson Coliseum?"

"Part of my job is preparing you to be a colleague, though, so I should say—"

"But," I interrupt, "you don't want me as a colleague."

He looks down wearily at the open pages. I regret that some of the doodles are in purple pen.

"I'm like a maid, but instead of your socks I pick up your species." I think this is pretty good, but his expression doesn't change. "Can we strike some kind of deal? You get me through this experience—write a decent evaluation, sign off on my thesis proposal—and I keep my head down and do the work?"

He looks up. "Is that some kind of threat?"

"A bargain is literally the opposite of a threat."

"You volunteer to keep silent about my, what, *emotional abuse*?" He says it like it's some kind of twenty-first-century phrase invented by braless women. I have to stop talking to any men about flowers.

Valerianella carinata, keeled lamb's-lettuce

Called rapunzel. Edible spatulate leaves, the size of thumbs.

That first night, you didn't wake. If I was the prince climbing into your tower, you did not stir at my presence, nor toss me a ladder of your hair. I sat and watched the dark pass over your face in shades, the stars' slow movement reflected on your brow. Your mouth bore all the unguarded conviction mine never had. Awake, I was ever conscious, moving my lips in patterns to make meekness, womanliness, seduction, ignorance; I had performed my way out of my self. And yet there lay a girl whose lips were nothing but lips. Held nothing but flesh. Offered nothing at all. I leaned over them, to listen. No witch burst in to break the spell. I listened all night.

XXXI.

Compositae

Erigeron canadensis, Canada flea-bane

Compositae is the largest family represented in the Colosseum, per my notes, and also I think maybe the floweriest (daisies! daisies!), and though we mostly call it Asteraceae because botany is an evolving discipline and people (men) like giving old things new names, my advisor still thinks it's important for me to memorize Deakin's key on how to tell them all apart. What I have learned (I will write in my end-of-semester report, dutiful, nonthreatening) is that asters are funny because they have a pappus. This is how the key goes: Is the pappus hairy? Is it in a single row? A double row? Is the pappus awned? Absent? Is it a membranous margin? Is it wanting? Does it have cup-like scales? Sessile scales? Is it hairy or hairlike? If the pappus is hairy, how f-ing hairy is it?

"Can you define pappus?" he once asked me, his hands in his lap, like an awning for his membranous margin.

"It's the fuzz they scrape out of your lady box with a spear."

"No."

"It's a nipple, used for feeding babies who grow in your lady box if it's not scraped all the way out."

"That's not—"

"It's the soft food you give to babies after your nipples start bleeding and you no longer want your skin torn with dagger teeth."

Women, women, women.

"It's a modified calyx—write it down, there—almost unique to Asteraceae, example: the carrier of dandelion seed," he said. "Pappus, two *p*'s."

"Three *p*'s."

"Write it down."

No, I don't call that emotional abuse. I call it humorlessness. The misogyny is a different matter.

I mail a postcard to my brother on the evening walk from work to home and realize I've told him nothing of this city. What matters outside the Colosseum? My bare apartment turns me gray; my advisor's office is a trap. The dusk buses blow past, and I can't make out the specificity of anything not green and growing. Sleep is the only travel I get. It's where I dream about plants I used to know and plants I want to know again.

Tussilago farfara, colt's-foot

I didn't come back to you the next night because I grew a racking cough. My mother gathered colt's-foot in the Forum, that pretty-headed flower, and dried the leaves above the fire so I might smoke them. I held a green one in my hand, downy, cobwebs above and cotton below, and thought of the hairs in the dip before your ears, that place where infant fur once grew and now is soft as a leaf. I didn't touch it—I defend myself in this telling though you may never return to challenge it, though it's the first time you hear it—I didn't touch your cheek that night because I knew better.

It was a relief then not to sleep. My cough kept me in consciousness of you, nine dark hours, or was it fourteen.

Senecio vulgaris, groundsel

The worst kind of weed—*troublesome*, Deakin calls it, sprouting in *ill-cultivated* places. Britain only lists five "injurious" plants in their 1959 Weeds Act: two thistles, two docks, and a *Senecio*. Like a Roman dandelion, cut-leafed, with pouching yellow rocket blooms, rayless, and a fuzzy poof of seed. *Senecio*, senescent, an old man, old-man-in-the-spring; vulgar. Yet canaries adore it, find this trouble most flavorful.

That's how I used to market myself. I was a tricky specimen, but nothing in nature goes uneaten. We've come to a stalemate, my advisor and I; the thought of him reading my notes, though he says he didn't, makes me nauseous. It's my fault, this feeling of violation—I'm the messy id-iot. But my brain has always been off-limits, and he's inside. What next? He could send me home. I could—

Another man in shorts drops his empty plastic sleeve of once-peanuts. The wind carries it under construction tape to me. I set it on fire with my eyes, and the smell catches his attention, makes him drop to his knees in apology to me, to God, to all the trash he once called women. The Colosseum ignites.

Inula, elecampane
I. odora, I. conyza, I. sordida

Elecampane grew where Helen of Troy's tears fell. Beauty begetting beauty. Or grief used for gain. I was ill for a sea-son, which explains my lost sense of time. I missed most the nightly sneaking, bringing back small treasures—ribbon, fish bone, root, ink—the meaning all mine. My room seemed to empty out.

My sister caught it too, and for a month we both teetered on the edge of nothing; this was the pinnacle of uselessness, of in-vanity. Women in bed, wearing white, coughing red. I made all the vows, even to God, and said I would never again be merely female; He must not have been listening, because

He can't have sanctioned that oath. My sister died instead. Untouched by man, and enviable.

Solidago virgaurea, common goldenrod

Strange, in the ubiquity of goldenrods, to find only one species here. Or rather, not find one. I put another line through Deakin's list. I imagine him running a bract of yellow flowers under his nose, recording its particularity in his notebook, in that feminine hand. Sometimes it's nice to imagine Deakin as a cross-dresser—a woman who wanted to fight in the wars of science and so tucked her hair in a cap and bound her breasts and carried a sword. Her mother at home weeping, her father flustered but proud; how could he not be, he who wanted a son? Only at night, sleeping in the trench's tight quarters with a dozen other botanists, does she worry about being found out: a hand thrown over her chest accidentally, a furtive peeing in the woods interrupted by a roving sentry. What's the punishment for a woman being a man?

Henry Ford thought gas had a short future, so he built cars out of soybeans, ran them on alcohol. To Thomas Edison he gave a special Model T with tires made from goldenrod. *A flower car*, I like to picture Ford saying winsomely, *from me to you*. Men with daisies, women in war.

Solidago leaves contain 7 percent rubber. We all have short futures.

FIG. 4

Pulicaria dysenterica, flea-bane

The sap smells to me of peaches. I make a note. Deakin is beginning to loosen, to allow more leeway in my floral narratives, or else he's starting to laze. I try to keep them brief and unromantic. Science, he tells me often, is knowledge freed from emotion. I wonder how many days or centuries it will take for him to be proven wrong.

A man walks by dragging a mule on a rope, the two of them bearing the same expression, one with a basket of squash, the other with a pannier of wheat. Their faces lost and resigned to loss. I'm surprised that within this jungle there's still room for kitchen gardens.

I drop the broken stem whose excretions I've inhaled and decide it's not the fleabane that smells of fruit but you. (You are not on my hands anymore, but my hands will not admit it.)

In the evenings I'm meant to bring a chaperone, this broken amphitheater being a lure for robbers, but I never do. Who will bring a man to defend against *me*?

Bellis, daisy
B. perennis, B. sylvestris

The Romans made daisy salves for their war wounds—*bellis*, from the root *bellum*.

"Or else they're just pretty, *bellus*," says the man with the pencil, who likes to question every fact I share. Didn't I say I'd shut up about plants?

We're at a Portuguese bar, a place that plays fado on Mondays, but it's Tuesday and the only distinguishing feature is some linguistic slurring. He has a hand on my knee, as if it were something good to hold. (There's no way it's anything more than a rung on the ladder upward; believe me, I've tried it, and it's like holding onto a rock, or an unripe grapefruit—no inherent value.)

"Four hundred and twenty species?" He mimes holding a joint between two fingers. I am sick to death, sick sick sick to death death death.

"Not anymore," I say. "He's working off a flora from 1855," carefully using *he* rather than *I* or *we*, "so I just have to see whether they're still present, and what else has come along in the meantime."

"And your advisor just sits in his office."

"Well, he writes grants. And yells at me."

"Has he ever made a pass?"

Sick to death. And yet I'm still sitting here on this barstool, aren't I?

"I once locked the door and exposed myself," I joke.

He doesn't blink.

"It was the only way I could get him to pay attention to the species we've lost. Just think: 1.8 degrees Fahrenheit over the past century. Of course things heated up will die."

My dead mother taught me how to make daisy chains by knotting their thin stems. She put their happy faces around my neck, as if she wouldn't ever perish. *Methinks that there abides in thee / Some concord with humanity*, Wordsworth said of the daisy. That doesn't make sense; their mood's too cheery. For concord, give me a thistle.

Bellium minutum, dwarf bellium

I thought it was a shrunken daisy, starved, lost in shadow, until I checked my taxonomies and learned it was just as it should be, though small.

Chrysanthemum leucanthemum, great white ox-eye

This is it, the largest, with buds that can be pickled like capers and dried leaves that smell of valerian—we've covered both of those, haven't we?—and a whiteness that's almost obscene; no plant should wear its race so baldly. It grows on tenacious rhizomes that can be hacked to bits by a farmer with a plow, and from each bit another daisy will grow.

When I was eighteen and fresh at college, when all I knew was that I hated science and loved boys, the volleyball coach pulled me by my ponytail into the locker room after practice and brushed that ponytail like it was a true horse's mane, sitting me down on the bench—blue, holed, that kind of steel covered in soft rubber—and taking his hand up the back of my neck and down my long thin hair, up and down, his great wet unblinking eye in my periphery. I didn't come to the next practice, or the next—just pretended I was dead—and at the season's first game there was another girl in my place.

I wonder if I write these things down so I might accidentally lose my journal again, and my advisor would learn what abuse really means, and why the long history of womanhood has me already spring-loaded for revenge.

Matricaria chamomile, wild chamomile

My mother said I slept more than my sister, and that's why I survived. But I have no recollection of sleeping at all. I could name every shadow that crossed the room from dusk to dawn, the spiders that spun corner webs and the cricket who snuck beneath the sill to play music at the foot of my bed. I imagined you walking through the night door a hundred times, your moonlight skin immediately familiar.

But my mother said she came into my room every night and touched my cheek and I did not stir. So maybe she was right, and sleep was better to me than waking and is what I remember.

I drank my chamomile, and my sister did not.

Anthemis, chamomile
A. cotula, A. mixta, A. tinctoria

One *Anthemis* is all-over yellow; another has oil-secreting glands along its stems that stink and burn the hands of anyone who tries to drag it out of a crop field. Pick your *Anthemis* wisely.

I took him home last night—yes, stupidly; no, he didn't have his pencil. It's hard to overstate the value of being paid attention to. He admired the smallness of my quarters, ran his hands over the row of copper pots—not mine—along the kitchen wall. Hardly anything in the apartment belonged to me. I thought about opening my suitcase, showing him my ball of underwear, a tangled necklace on the bathroom sink that I brought because I thought I'd have time for untangling. I *have* time, but I play games with men instead.

We sat on the sofa for long enough; I let him hold my knee like a handle. I felt like a human made up of handles.

"I'm surprised you don't have flowers here," he said, looking around at bare spaces, unwashed dishes.

"Flowers aren't really my thing," I said, which as long as he didn't know about my dead mother wouldn't be a lie. As long as he thought I only rummaged in the Colosseum for university credit. *Cold indeed must be the heart that does not respond to their silent appeal*, Deakin wrote in the *Flora*'s preface. I leaned over and put my head in his lap, as childlike as I could, which is what I wanted.

Every few years, I get what I want.

Bidens tripartita, bur marigold

The *tripartita* is one of the more ungainly beggar-ticks, with hardly a flower to speak of, just a brownish collection of petal stumps that looks like something waiting to bloom.

Last night, my soldier made his declarations (to my father), and I have been instructed (by my father) to accept. I struggle to envision all the days to come. I am conditioned to my servitude and, yes, the freedom in labor. But my master isn't Deakin but the green world. How much I've grown to need this Colossal landscape! It has all the fresh air of theft and none of the morning shame.

The scene appears to me: a close house, smoke-smelling, dried fish on chipped plates, a soldier in boots—ignoring me, which I wouldn't like, or asking things of me, which I wouldn't like. My chest trapped in whalebone, my feet in thin-soled shoes. Where would I go? To the window? Press my nose to the glass like a sailor's widow, waiting for the first sheen of the prow of the boat that'd bring you home. A ghost boat, surely; you still have not written.

Did you quake when you learned you were to be bound? If so, I never saw it. You said that having a husband was a relief, that there was value in being sure. Sure of what?

I stood over the Tiber when I heard your news and leaned like corn in the wind. Death was a weed waving at the bottom, and it looked very sweet to me—that was sureness. You were a coward. We were both cowards to stay in our bodies.

Achillea ageratum, sweet maudlin

He floats, a ghost, above the Colosseum. The bodies below are small and provoke in him no emotion. No maudlin, no yarrow, no sweet nancy. He thinks of a pretty girl, simple of scent, of style. No simple girl ever crossed his path, only maudlins. They are bloated with words. He slips into a thunderstorm, sends his fury out in bolts of light. He wanted a heaven of only men.

Eupatorium cannabinum, hemp agrimony

A pink fuzziness, called holy rope; for hanging? For tying saints together? Unclear, but the word is if you lay the leaves on bread, you can stave off mold for a day or two. Brutally hot today, but what a relief to find these puffs of mist skirting a low stone wall; I nearly sink my face into them. *Yes*, I mark on Deakin's list; *holy rope survives.* I snap their inconsequence with my phone's camera, my blurry finger half-occluding. If God indeed sends signs through weather, maybe a devout botanist should check to see which plants He's saving in the planet's slow boil. Holy rope, but not Christ's thorn?

I'm no theologian, but damnation sounds more likely than redemption.

I'm wearing a blue top, sleeveless, translucent (see above re: weather), and a man with a cap shifts on his feet a few yards distant, trying to find the angle at which the light will best penetrate my shirt. Should I stand? Should I shroud myself? Should I cannibalize?

My brother texts: "Home for Thanksgiving?"

It's more than a month away. "Hell no." I skulk behind some caution tape so I'm out of his sight line; no cannibalizing today. Just need some peace.

"Learning a lot?"

Something in me leaps whenever he asks me about myself. Little sister syndrome. "Yeah kinda."

"Whoring it up?"

Oh right. Ha ha.

"Ha ha," he texts quickly.

"Looking for a spouse I can abandon in a few years," I reply. "Ha ha."

"She says I get a pass now."

"The counselor??"

"No."

"Is that real?" I ask.

"Do you think so?"

I don't understand why anyone would ask me for relationship advice. "TRAP?"

"Yeah."

"I mean, do you want to?" I try to picture the women in his office: receptionists, one other mid-level type, none of them really my cup of tea, but obviously I'm not the customer. Do some people set out to cheat without a cheating partner in mind?

He hasn't responded.

"Look, I can't think about this stuff too much or I'll swear off relationships. So gross."

"I want stability," he writes.

Oh. I sympathize, I do. But what *I* want is jet propulsion. I want my aimless fleeing to tip over into determined chasing. And I'm starting to feel it. It's close.

"I'm sorry," I write. A blanket statement. "You do you."

He texts the palm-in-the-face emoji.

Chrysocoma linosyris, flax-leaved goldy-locks

It was at my sister's funeral we finally met. Not in your room, which I'd visit a dozen times more, but in the black echoing space of the church, our bodies both surviving the test of the narthex, seated in pews. Surrounded by the women of good repute, all weeping like cut stems. How many married, how many turning from their husbands in the night to shield their soil, to keep from making more girls who would catch sick and die, girls who if pretty would be touched and if plain would wither? A church of women, all looking down, no longer waiting for Christ.

Your hair bobbed golden, flaxen, white and yellow, wild sun in the dark.

Artemisia, wormwood
A. vulgaris, A. argentea

I put cut stalks of wormwood and him, both, in a bath, and settle in among the smells like Cleopatra. He wanted to cook for me, but I didn't want to be shown-off-at, which is why we're in swimsuits, like cousins.

"But Cleopatra bathed in milk."

"Calm down," I say.

He sticks a furry leg out, tries to feel along my hip with a foot. I lace my fingers in his hairs like reins. A silver spray of *Artemisia* floats along my skin, feathery.

"Is this, like, mint?"

"Is this *like* mint?" I clarify. "Or—"

He claws me with a toenail.

"Known as felon herb, old Uncle Henry, old-man, naughty-man."

"You're joking."

"Look at what it's done to me. Drugged me into misbehavior."

"You don't take your own life seriously, do you?"

I too am trying to place the scent—not mint or sage, but something more like aniseed. I close my eyes, thinking I can hear better that way, smell better, if I tune out his bare shoulders floating like islands above the water, sinking as inevitably as the Maldives.

"You don't even want to do what you're doing," he says.

"How do you know what I want?"

He moves his underwater hand up my leg. I could tell him all about my plans, the formal proposal I started drafting, the articles I downloaded on southeastern U.S. floras and ruderal zones and emotional memory in the limbic system, but my future to me is too precious for sharing.

When he grows old will all his hairs turn gray? Is there a verb for that, and if there isn't, can it be *to artemiege*, rhymes with *liege*? Who will be there to watch us after love has gone, when silver sets in? Is this what people want?

Filago, filago
F. gallica, F. minima, F. germanica

Why do I so love downy plants? My mother used to say, her hand on my belly, that they remind us of children. But they remind me of the back of your neck. One species of filago is the daggerleaf cotton rose, and this too makes me think of you, though it's too unwieldy for a daily endearment. It rises in thin spikes from dry soil, covered in down, in what we call pubescence, and there you are before me, unclothed, your black weeds gone and nothing but your softness and your shocking golden hair.

"What of me do you treasure most?" you once teased, lying beside me, heat rising.

I was still shrouded in my shift. I believed you were wilder than any man. "This," I said, and hovered my mouth an inch above your heart.

"How strange." You laughed and flipped onto your stomach and a new landscape emerged. "I've been praised by men, but what they adored was the thought of touching—and here you are: I offer you this whole shape, and yet!"

I couldn't touch you for the thorns. It wasn't shame, but fear of how much it would hurt, that pleasure.

"Do you want to know what it feels like?" you said. You lifted my shift up to my neck, took my hand, and placed it on my breast. "Here," you said. You took back your hand, put it on your own chest. You moved it down to the curve of your waist; I did the same. You smoothed over the hill of your hip; I did the same. Down the side of your thigh, I mirroring you, and up the inner skin. I could not believe I could feel so soft, or look so lovely. You moved your hand to mine, and I, who'd been so bold, became as shy as butter, and let you come.

Calendula arvensis, field marigold

A yellow-blooming spray, lanceolate leaves; fills the Italian meadows with reasons to celebrate. A girl picking a bouquet would have to go out of her way to avoid the marigold. A woman here stoops to add one to her guidebook: *Rzym*. She tucks it among the *kościoły* and *muzea*, a yellow spot that when she revisits it in Gdańsk will be brown, as faded as a memory. "What did you see?" her father will ask. "What was most beautiful?" And the churches with their Caravaggios will blur, the Tiber will become a pond, and the only color she can definitively name is the salmon of a woman's dress as it swept by her café table in the square—some square. "Tell me of the emperors, at least," he'll say, spectacled, and she'll open the guidebook to the page with the flattened *Calendula*, and her father's eye will land on it with suspicion: he is brought to mind of a summer in his youth, when he won a girl's promise with a wreath. His response to his own shame is anger.

Isn't it funny that I might remember this moment of her, stooping in the Colosseum, better than she ever will? Even though hers is not my life?

Carlina corymbosa, carline thistle

I wear a thistle in my dress when I dine with him alone (my parents in the parlor just beyond, murmuring; an old lady with her needlework, chaperoning, asleep in the chair by the sideboard, where the Cornish hens were laid). Not the carline thistle, with its brilliant explosions of gold set in copper involucres, like a weapon slowly catching on fire, but the mild lavender kind, which could be confused for a sweet bloom at a distance. The distance is the thing.

I ask the soldier what he thinks of unification, stroking my spines. He has progressed past the hens to the sponge cake and is licking his fork with a bearish tongue. At my words, he pauses, drops the fork, fumbles in his jacket, and across the wooden table rolls a ring at me. It clatters to a stop by my glass; the old lady jumps in her sleep.

"I meant Italy," I say.

He jerks to his feet and circles the table to get to me. I bring a hand up to my chest, ready to wield my brooch. He drops to his knees, eyes wide as childhood.

"Tell me what I may do for you," he says.

Carduus, thistle
C. pycnocephalus, C. leucographus, C. marianus

"Tell me what I can do to you," he says.

Out of the bath, his hand on my breast.

C. marianus is the Marian thistle, the milk thistle, its leaves stained white with drops of milk from the nursing Mary. Deakin calls it a *blessed stain*. I sometimes have trouble imagining him as a man, this botanical forebear. He could be so gentle with these specimens, so yielding to their charms. So f-ing sensitive. I wish someone would walk into this sordid bedroom and make a cross on my forehead with their thumb and whisper through the fog of longing, *I bless your stain.*

FIG. 5

Lappa major, burdock

A problematic plant: bristly, yet edible. As blindingly purple as the firmament, yet weedy. Its leaves, which children avoid, shelter snails. When burned, it lays down its nutrients onto crop fields, furnishing them with alkaline salts.

"Is not this a lesson for our own mortal souls?" Deakin asks. His desk is crowded with seedpods I have brought him, and turtle shells he's found on his own. He has plans to make them into rattles for his nieces.

"That we too may treat with both the saints and the Devil?"

He tilts his head at me. "No," his hand on a shell. "That in dying our flesh shall be made into different matter and offer sustenance to the next spring of man."

"Your nieces' nieces wait for you, then."

He doesn't hear me, but moves his hand to the dried burdock heads. "Cumbersome," he says. He repeats the word, trying to reconcile it with this new definition of faith.

Centaurea, knapweed
C. nigra, C. cyanus, C. calcitrapa, C. solstitialis

Bluebottle, cornflower, star thistle, cockspur. I like my weeds tall. In parts of the U.S. where they don't like their weeds tall or short or any whichway in between, some know-it-alls have released weevils, gallflies, and peacock flies to lay their eggs in star-thistle flowers, so the baby bugs can gnaw their way out through seed. And yet knapweed feeds the goldfinch, the honeybee, the painted lady. The smoothest of them all: *C. cyanus*, the bachelor's button, tended by women in garden beds and raised to be beloved.

It doesn't do well in Mississippi, but where I've seen it growing (not here, in this baking Roman bowl, but in Englands both old and New), its blue has sent a cold arrow through my veins. It's the color of armies—Prussian, Swedish, Austrian—and of Romantics. Vermeer and Novalis. It's bottomless, that blue. (The secret is having no trace of green; if you're going to be something, be *all* something.) My suicide plan—we all have one—is to fall into the depths of a cornflower.

"Flowers weren't made for poets," my advisor says, "but bees." His eyes slip down to my chest again.

He hasn't read my full proposal yet; he can't ethically reject it until he does. (As for ethics, oh the letter I could write to the chair of his department!) I sense we're both suiting up for battle. Until the draft's ready, all I can do is practice hearing his *no* in my head, so I take every opportunity to provoke him.

"I am a bee," I say. And then, "I heard you're turning this fieldwork into an article. Will my name be on it?"

It's too soon; my journal is fresh in his mind. He digs around in his ear. "You'll certainly be acknowledged."

"A footnote."

"Scholarship is interpretation, reflection. That's my job."

"Do you ever wonder about Deakin? What kind of help he had, or whether he did all the writing himself? I mean, he was British, right; they knew how to find unpaid labor."

He rubs his eyes. He's running out of orifices. "I don't question authorship."

Author, authority. From *auctor*, father. "Some of his phrases strike me as feminine."

His face brightens. "Ah! But I thought *language* shouldn't be *gendered*."

He's not petty; he's just so f-ing old.

Hypochaeris radicata, long-rooted cat's-ear

A false dandelion, the trick of which can be discovered in the stem, true dandelion stalks being hollow rather than solid.

After the funeral I found you in the churchyard holding a bouquet of weeds.

"I'm sorry for your sister," you said, passing it over.

I don't know how I didn't touch your hand in this exchange—I considered it nightly, how a hand could give another hand a collection of loose flowers without flesh touching (did I purposefully clasp just under the flower heads, so as to avoid your fingers farther down? Did you release your grip a second before my own took hold?)—but you left without contact, like a sun passing over the cloud.

My mother said your father was our doctor's banker, a

tenuous tie, but later I learned you begged him to attend the funeral because you were curious about death.

Chondrilla juncea, gum succory

I wasn't one of those buxom junior high girls with figures nearly toppling their small bodies, who for a few years look like balloon versions of themselves. This nearly saved me: not having anything to grab on to. I could stand behind telephone poles and vanish. But there aren't enough girls to go around—not anywhere.

Skeletonweed, nakedweed, devil's grass.

It's just a matter of time.

Picris hieracioides, hawkweed picris

I ask for ten days to consider my position. (I would have asked for seven, it seeming a more mythical number, but it wasn't long enough—what I really wanted was seventy, or seven hundred.) The soldier acquiesces with all the politeness of a man pretending to be in love.

"He *does* love you," my father says, and I agree that in their definition of it, yes. I have all my teeth and am under thirty.

The first night my father makes no arguments, and my mother passes silently from room to room with a pot of tea, waiting to be needed.

The second night I slip out from the open window after the stars have been lit, a route I haven't taken since you sailed. A man lies on the street with bread in his hand, uneaten, a dog with its head propped on his feet. Another man in velvet coat stumbles forward, his hand feeling along the houses to find which way is up. A night guard carries a torch, pays attention to no one. I've learned to wear pants.

I wander toward St. Peter's, toward finer homes, and find myself outside the soldier's house. A pipe runs from the roof to the cobbles, and with my feet in the cracks of old stone, I clamber to an upstairs window, slip in. His mother and father are asleep in their bed. I walk on the sounds of their snores to what must be his room: musket, coat, boots, spittoon. There's no body there. No body for me to sit beside and wonder over. No ear on which to dwell. No down.

He's a man; he must be searching for another woman.

Picris means *bitter*.

Taraxacum officinalis, dandelion

He floats, a ghost, above the Colosseum. His teeth ache from the violence done him. Little lion's teeth, *dents de lion*, dandelion. Roots fat and milky, roots like breasts, petals toothed, teething on breasts. Who can look at weeds and not see women? Is it his fault his world made no allowances for them? He tries to descend on the blood-soaked soil, but the wind currents, cold at night, keep him aloft.

Thrincia hirta, hairy thrincia

Listen to Deakin again, try not to fall for his sensual attention: *root, abrupt. Leaves, all radical. Sinuated in a runcinate
manner. Smooth above, hairy below. Downy on the margin.*

I built myself a calciferous shell after my dead mother
died. If I'd had breasts to bind, I would've bound them. I
started off goth, all-black everything, caked swoops around
my eyes, stomped. Even when no one was home, I stomped
from bedroom to bathroom, on the assumption that what?
Someone was listening? My echoing feet made the loud
sounds my mouth couldn't. My father turned in on himself;
my brother went driving. I was what was left of her, banging
around in a hollow house. Her garden shriveled to nothing.
I wanted nothing kept alive.

And yet in sleep I dreamed, like a little girl, of fairies.
Downy on the margin.

Cichorium intybus, wild succory

We are drinking coffee, the four of us—man, man, man, and
me—or rather to set the scene in its just light, I am pouring
a pot of hot chicory into porcelain cups, each painted with
an indeterminate blue flower (perhaps cornflower, perhaps
gentian; it could be the Blue Flower itself, whose indeter-
minacy is the reason male artists so cleave to the image—
though they pin down emotions, sterilizing them like moths

on a mount, they won't admit to flowers being science, or children being humans, or women's art being real). I do not give myself a blue-flowered cup, consumption being unseemly. My father speaks to the soldier's father while the soldier keeps his eyes on his own brown boots, and I gently arrange the pot and the sugar and the spoons and the cream, making fractal patterns. The gray-haired men remember their own romances, though what they are speaking of is property and profession.

The soldier swirls his cup and whispers, *"Me pascunt olivae, me cichorea, me malvae."*

I pity him.

"Horace," he says. "I feed on olives, chicory."

"Mallow," I say.

I've told Deakin of the marriage, and he said, *Well that's an end to it*, and I didn't say no, a married woman too could prostrate herself in age-old dirt, dig for roots and bite bitter leaves and make her markings in a book. I'm a radical, but I'm not a fool.

When I tell you of the marriage, will you say, *Well that's an end to it?* I am a fool, imagining the end didn't happen long ago.

They leave their cups with a wet dust of chicory inside. *Cichorium* roots are blanched and ground, the leaves harvested early for spring salads, the flowers—beautiful, blinding blue—are left cut, to wither.

Lactuca, lettuce
L. muralis, L. saligna, L. scariola

Did you know if you can stomach the bleeding milk from wilting *Lactuca* leaves, they'll numb your pain, *a drowsy numbness pains / my sense*, as though of lettuce I had drunk? Like opium, but better side effects.

I'm not in a place in my life that hosts depression. I'm years past the dead mother, years past the most recent mauling, I am in *Rome*, I am breeding freedom, full from feeding on sun and art and cheese and flower. I'm feeling possessive of my plants, I'm spinning a man into *my* web, and my shoulders are finally browned. So what in these salad days can I possibly regret? Why do I want to yank the lettuce that doesn't look like lettuce at all out of the amphitheater's stone walls and wait for it to age so I can numb my undeserved meek wallowing pain?

I pick up my pen again. I flip past the pages of angry scrawls. I write, *Flora Colisea: Jackson*. The cattails in the pond near my house were my favorite plant as a child, brown and whistling with red-winged blackbirds. The pond is gone; it became a football field. Could I slow my town's unrolling ruin by naming what exists? Is that what we're doing here with these lists, slowing death?

Sonchus, sow-thistle
S. oleraceus, *S. tenerrimus*

S. oleraceus must be distinguished from *S. tenerrimus*—one being a floral sun exploding in eight concentric bursts, the other in a sedate three; one having ovate fruit, the other triangular; a smooth involucre versus one woolly at its base; called *common*, called *clammy*; one delighted upon by asses, the other crowning St. Peter's. Two sides of a genus, a plant that any ordinary passerby would fail to notice or, if noticed, would call a dandelion.

No, there is no point to distinguishing them.

Except—the only lesson I carry from Deakin—every thing deserves its name.

Crepis, hawk's-beard
C. biennis, *C. pulcher*

"You're not a very sympathetic person," the man with the pencil says in another bar, this one Russian. I've gotten used to the hand-on-knee phenomenon; I just numb the knee in my mind, give it one good shot of anesthetic.

"You mean I don't sympathize with others, or I myself don't elicit sympathy?"

He leans in and kisses me on the cheek, which is what he does when a situation needs neutralizing.

I realize I've approached this person—tentatively, and

also with belligerence—as someone who will inevitably hurt me. And yet, I date him not because I'm a masochist but because it's nice to be seen, even when the seer has no idea what you are. (All my little weeds are wagging assent.) So can I just put down my f-ing weapons for a night?

Against the discordance of Russian house music, he tells me it was at his ninth birthday party that his little brother found his father's gun and blew off his own foot, and that he didn't have any birthday parties after that, or a father (his mom sent him and his gun packing), and how until his brother got a prosthetic he (my man) promised he'd walk with him to school and then instead would run so fast he'd leave the broken boy behind.

I reluctantly recognize the grief in masculinity. They were as little prepared for the world as we were overprepared.

The *Crepis*es at the Colosseum are entirely different species from what Deakin saw (*C. setosa*, *C. vesicaria*, *C. bursifolia*, *C. sancta*)—proof that survival has always required change. But who would really know without careful looking, without the kind of looking so close it begins to hurt.

Hieracium, hawkweed
H. murorum, *H. nestleri*, *H. pilosella*

I came again to your room after my sister's funeral, now that I knew what your open eyes were like. I took your rings, your hairbrush, your hanging gown, your *Pilgrim's Progress*, your glass of water, your scent.

I left in their place the dried weeds you'd given me. (Some. Some I'd saved.) Among them was a hawkweed, which old shepherds thought falcons fed on to sharpen their vision. (Can you see it? The young hawk kneeling in the grass, nibbling at the meadow, fortifying itself before a hunt for hare?) I ate one bloom and stared more closely at you, and yes, I could count your lashes.

But hawkweed also sends poison from its roots to clear the soil of competitors.

Is this what I did when I emptied your room?

Not empty; I left the weed. You said when you woke and saw the plant, you knew.

Lapsana communis, nipple-wort

Okay, let's just agree this one needs a new name. Even by 1855, Deakin admits that while *Lapsana* was once smeared on sore breasts, *it is now quite out of use.* The buds look like nipples, is all. It's the doctrine of signatures, this unswerving belief that God in His just design gave us plants with their uses painted clearly on. Lungwort, liverwort, toothwort, eye-bright. Walnuts for headaches, because don't they look like little brains? I only wonder why He didn't make our own faces broadcast our potential and our limits. What my brother said after his first date with my rosy-cheeked sister-in-law:

She looks *like a wife*. I can interpret. Docile, wide of hip, finds all jokes funny. And now?

"She says she never wanted kids!"

"Whoa!" I text, not feeling any surprise at all. "You're killing it in therapy, huh?"

"Feels like starting over."

"Lucky."

My advisor refuses to call *Lapsana* by its common name; this too makes my skin twitch. I *do* feel bad for men some days.

Zacintha verrucosa, warted zacinth

With lyrate leaves, shaped like those instruments of old. I wonder at their purpose. If they are accompanying songs too green for us to hear. If this is a signature of God to mark our deafness.

XXXII

Dipsaceae

Knautia arvensis, field knautia

An electric-violet pincushion flower, a kind of scabious, so called because they used to rub it on skin (oh, my long-suffering medieval woman!) to cure plague, scabies, *scabere* meaning to scratch.

My dead mother told me not to pick at scabs. But here I am, red-cheeked in the office of a man who's fed up with me, finally floating my research project, a *Flora Colisea*.

"Yet another?" my advisor says, eyes pricked with self-preservation.

"Of a different Colisea," I say. I tell him about the Col-osseum I grew up with, the Coliseum in Jackson, the once yellow-sided, now mirror-sided big top where the circus came and sometimes Bobby Rush, where you went for the science fair, for graduation, for monster trucks. Its 6,500 seats proffered up for the Dixie National Rodeo, its circularity poised atop the crater of the Jackson Volcano, its livestock barns radiating out like petals.

"The Colosseum seated fifty thousand."

"Bully for you," I say.

He laughs, a laugh from the gut, at what must, *must*, have been my joke. The country-fried flora, the girl with her own research agenda, the girl with a gun.

"Flora have usually been written with a plan of discovery," he says, and everything has to twist so hard inside me to prevent a spewing-forth of anti-colonialist rage.

"Self-discovery is something scientists could use more of, don't you think?"

"And so the expectation is that I will approve this—I don't want to say childish fancy, but shall we call it underdeveloped?—underdeveloped proposal, and you will leave in December without having accused me of whatever wrongs you have stored in your quiver?"

"My quiver?"

He pantomimes pulling an arrow from behind his back and aiming it at me.

"I mean, if you want to tell me how to be smarter, I'd welcome that, but it doesn't seem like that's your goal." I think of him reading my notes, my anger, my weakness, my dick doodles. I wonder what it would feel like to have a mentor. A man who wasn't an adversary. A mother.

He runs his hands across his desk, considering. "Mississippi, then, is it? And here I thought you'd grown up and left home behind."

So the plan is to belittle me.

Scabiosa columbaria, small scabious

The flower is actually a burst of flowers. What presents as a single bloom is, upon inspection, a parade of smaller beauties. The soldier and I stroll, trailed by an old woman hired by his family to play the grandmother. Even a reluctant pairing needs a chaperone, the human instinct for trouble being rooted in lust. Lust sprouting from difference. (For those who do not know self-love, do not know what glory lies in one's own form, mirrored in another.) He does make a move toward my hand. The grandmother coughs. Two benches receive us, an obelisk finishing the triangle. On her bench, the grandmother nods toward her feet; on ours, we stare at the hieroglyphs. Again, he chases my palm with a pinky. I let him raise it up, inspect my fingers, the nails backlit by dirt. He says nothing. Not *My wife can have no profession*, neither *Tell me what you do*. Lets the hand go. It may be that in our speechlessness we are both thinking of other women: he of his mistress—uncontestedly extant, surely willing—me of mine, her body buoyed by an ocean, over a soundless deep, too deep to be sounded, too dark to make sound. When you said *honeymoon*, did you consider all the bees that would starve when you went so far?

I should keep the florets of your beauty with me while swallowing the florets of this present. Man, grandmother, obelisk, soil beneath my nails. A good human would treasure the gone and the come. Where is the human instinct for goodness?

XXXIII.

Cucurbitaceae

Bryonia dioica, red-berried bryony

He floats, a ghost, above the Colosseum. He hunts the violent-berried bush, the violet violent berries, belly-purging, throat-squeezing, gut-spilling. Its root as big as a child, newborn, pale and crinkled. He would never put his seed in a woman; they're lying if they claim it. May any baby's innards be twisted, instinct be wrenched. When he spits from his height, it's borne away before it reaches any earth. Even now, he nourishes nothing.

Momordica elaterium, squirting cucumber

Here's how it works: the ripe pod, gently brushed, drops from the stem; the sides of the triggered fruit contract, squeezing the seeds out through a hole left by the stem; the seeds, covered in mucus, go shooting out all over; and the milkmaids are delighted. It happens fast as a rocket, but there are videos online that slow it down to pornographic speed—jets of liquid, hydrant hoses, spewing tiny black bits. Those signature-believers decided it must be an abortifacient, so ruthlessly did it eject seed. In fact, in high doses, it can kill a man.

XXXIV

Campanulaceae

Campanula rotundifolia, round-leaved bell-flower

How different a harebell looks growing loose in waves on the English moor, or singly sprouting through errant cracks in city stone. Do you bloom differently on your boat than you did in my arms? (*In my arms* being a romantic phrase, suggesting stillness, compliance, that bears no relation to what we were.) Crouched in this place busy with green, hands full with notebook, pencil, collecting sack, hair pulled into tangles by shrubs, am I most perfectly myself? No. The old Romans simulated wildness here, staging *silvae* with false trees, false flowers so the hordes could see what the city had erased. They applauded, even when nothing died.

I want to think your letters have been stolen; I would suspect my parents, except they've built me a future so ironclad, they must believe no small roots of longing could crack the contract. But I also can't mistrust you. Love dies, but it does not evaporate. I accuse the gulls—some raucous birds have taken your missives in their beaks and digested them along with herring. I blame nature for its savagery; I hide within it, in the chaos of the Colosseum. My father has not told the soldier where to find me in the day. I have not been accosted by the shepherds and the kitchen gardeners, the afternoon drunkards and the prayerful. The darts of brown across my cheek and brow deter. I am not merely unladylike, but un-human. I am becoming vegetative, and flowers, despite the metaphors, have no true flesh to be plucked.

Wahlenbergia, wahlenberga
W. erinus, W. hederacea

The ivy-leaved bellflower has pursed its lips. Or narrowed its eyes—at any rate, it doesn't explode on the vine like its larger cousin but offers just its outer edges of blue. I'm supposed to be improving my leaf ID skills, learning to describe them as cordate rather than just drawing girlish hearts in my notes. My advisor narrows his lips when he says this, when he sees my paper—he purses his eyes.

"You know botany involves science," he says.

"I only know what my professors teach me," I say.

Wahlenbergia famously beautified the Fountain of Egeria, where the kings of Rome consulted with bodiless nymphs, those bellflowers like ladies *which gracefully / Bend their small heads in every breeze*. From the grottoes to the bloody circus.

The Jackson Coliseum had circuses too. Tigers, elephants. In the concrete skirt around its wide mirrored middle, weed grass grows.

"What grass?" he says.

Weed grass, and city-skinny crape myrtles, and purple-leaved *Loropetalum*, and a single sycamore, its seed dropped too close to a column, shooting up its side in a nervous cling. A woman with wide hands, wide breasts, wide hips, flattening herself in desperation beside something immovable. *Who's she fooling*, the viewer says, pursing, narrowing.

I consider how my dead mother would laugh to hear of my thesis idea, to think anything in Jackson worth examination. She felt trapped there. Maybe she was waiting for my father to die so she could burst free, go back to school, move to Budapest. But Jackson is the only place I knew her. She came from a cabbage leaf; she sprang from the sea. So I have both men and ghosts to prove wrong. Easy.

Jasione montana, sheep's-bit

Root, simple. Leaves, linear. Flowers, stalked. My first letter to you was like this. Salutation *dear*, content dreary, postscript guaranteed. I was so ashamed of my deficiencies I mailed it in the dirt, covering it in a hole beneath your window's twining grapevine.

Two days later I received a response, perfumed with freesia, at my father's door.

This is all that ever needs to be told of the two of us: that we were buried and still bloomed.

Prismatocarpus speculum, Venus's looking glass

My father took me to a gynecologist when I was sixteen because I was f-ing volcanic with acne and either he was grossed out or my dead mother left him a note with a basic timeline for raising girls. (Period; pustulating face; prom.)

The doctor was old white-haired man with powder-dry hands and yellowing nosepads on his spectacles. It wasn't spectacles he put up me, but what he called *Venus's looking glass*. (Should I have clawed at the door to get out?) A metal tongue that opened and closed like a castanet, mirrored, so the goddess of love could be reflected back at me. Except of course I was wedged up in a hinge, my privates kept private from me behind a paper sheet—the looking glass only reflected him. I made some teenage joke to that effect, and his face raised above my curtained knees like a breaching whale, the spectacles turning his eyes fishy and bubbled.

The tongue still stretched in my privates.

"Has Cupid," he said, "struck you with his arrow?"

XXXV

Stellatae

Galium, bed-straw
G. verum, G. cruciatum, G. mollugo,
G. parisiense, G. aparine

My sheets are prickled with *Galium* seeds, which hook on with weedy courage as I, climbing to the higher stone altitudes, brush by their bushes. At night I roll them off me in my dreams. Bedstraw, mugweed, goosegrass, cleavers. The Greeks took this dispersal pattern for love and named the plant *Philanthropon*. There are a hundred plants I'd name *Philanthropon* for the way they draw me, hook me, swoon me, subdue me. Not *Galium*, though, which tangles my bed and jabs the skin at the backs of my knees.

We have a woman who takes our sheets at the end of the month to whatever sunnier home she owns, and after two days of sleeping on bare mattresses, we welcome back their country smells with minor celebrations. Since I began my botanical study, she's refused my linens, there being too much plant matter in them. She was raised in Umbria, near my grandmother's people, where a leaf could be God's poison and a crooked seed was a message from the Devil.

My father said I can wash my own, so I don't. I sleep in cleavers; they remind me I'm not in the bed I once visited.

Vaillantia muralis, wall-vallantia

The man with the pencil helps me today; he sticks grass stems in my ear while I crawl around the northern perimeter fondling calyxes. I said it'd be deadly dull (read: *Please don't come*), but he said, "You don't want me?" and though I didn't, no one had taught me how to say that and survive, so now I have grass twiddling in my ear as I'm trying to do my f-ing job.

The *Valantia*, which Deakin, in a continental flourish, called *Vaillantia*, is one of those species that survived: small, tough, weaselly, and brutish. Short spikes of leaves swirling out of a rosette base, the leaves alternating with a kind of freaky burrlike growth—maybe it's part of the leaf too, or a seedpod, or just an alien excrescence? Like baby flytraps, or sea slugs.

"Is that the flower?" he asks.

I laugh before I can catch myself—how stupid can men be?—and then am stricken with doubt. *Is it the flower??*

"No," I say, certainty outmatching truth.

I've begun planning my ivory tower attack, so I'm collecting lessons—the more questionable the better. If my advisor's going to take me down, he's going to take me down swinging.

"Here's a two-cheeked rose," the man with the pencil says, poking my butt with his shoe.

Rubia tinctorum, dyer's madder

There are plants with invisible value. The madder stems bear whorls of leaves with prickles reflexed around the margins; the flowers bloom meekly, in shrunken yellows. It would take an aggrieved weeder to dig it up and find the pearl: vast tuberous roots, three to four feet long, fat and glowing red.

To get the dye, the roots are cleaned and baked, muddled and mixed with fixers, alum and ammonia and acid. For Turkey red, the cloth is dipped in spoiled olive oil and sheep's dung, then alum, madder, calf's blood, and washed with tin. Repeat, repeat. Animals who feed on madder grow red bones.

Red was needed for war, for the British coats that marched on America (each murmuring *madder*), and equally for religion, a milder saffron that tinted hermits' robes. And red was swallowed by women, some to make their courses come, others to stop the lives clawing inside them. To make the courses come back.

You'd had a child put in you once and let it go. Not *lost*, for you knew all along where it was. This was why you bristled at my yearning.

Sherardia arvensis, blue sherardia

Like madder, but nicer, violet.

"What if it's not blooming and you can't tell what color it is?"

"It's in season," I say. "It's blooming." I scrabble at sticky leaves looking for the tiny bastards.

"What if a little girl came along and picked all the flowers?"

"She'd be an idiot. They're, like, three millimeters big."

"Maybe she has little hands."

I sit back on my heels and look at his face, broad and sunny, an overhang of golden eyebrows. It takes him four hours a day to do his full-time job, and I assume he gets paid six figures. And he's talking about kids. I find men don't tend to mention them unless they're starting to reach those philosophical crises of age and are connecting (subconsciously) the width of your hips with the immortality of their name.

"If I saw a girl picking my flowers, I'd drop-kick her," I say.

He makes a note.

I scratch in my book *Sherardia absent*, and hope it's because it really doesn't exist anymore, wiped out by rising temperatures and bouquet-mad children, and not because I just missed it, a guy nattering away in my ear.

Asperula odorata, sweet woodruff

It breathes sweetness. I brush against it with my skirts and it exhales. The white petals, star-shaped, bend back as if caught in a wind of its own scent. I lean to catch its words. *Press me to your breast*, it says, *and I will keep away the moths*.

The Colosseum is gray today, swamped in clouds and cool. A woman kneels before one of the country altars. She prays to St. Agnes, places on the stone a spray of goldenrod. I have never stopped at one of the shrines here to make a plea, not in all my days caught in this strange prison. I have knelt so much among the weeds that another genuflection seems gluttonous. I tell God to tend to the seeker at St. Agnes's station instead. I remain comfortable with the reins of my destiny.

The wedding is set for the winter. I dumbly predict you'll have returned by then, that marriage will not have suited you and you will come to save your thief. By then the flowers I am hunting will have died back and my list—his list—will be done.

XXXVI

Caprifoliaceae

Sambucus ebulus, dwarf elder

One of those toxic growths with a dozen spooky names, *danewort*, *daneweed*, *danesblood*. It's because it only grows on battlefields where Danes spilled blood (how can this possibly be true, what Dane was slain in New Jersey?), or because *dane* once meant diarrhea, which is what would happen if you gorged yourself on those shiny black berries. I put asterisks by the poisonous plants—you know, in case.

Small white flowers in drifts, anthers painted nail-polish pink. The smell has been called *foetid*.

My dead mother used to rub the leaves of *Sambucus canadensis* on my child arms to scare the mosquitoes, who chuckled and set to work. Our native cousin never struck me as vile, as *foetid*, as hiding purgative depths. But I was young, hadn't yet wanted so badly to vomit.

Viburnum tinus, laurestine

We built a house beneath your bed, like a womb. You worried about the night nurse (your mother had produced her last infant), so we barricaded the dark with pillows, a bedskirt, the blankets pulled under and no nub of a candle. In our new home we were too close, too blind to see each other. Your hair in my mouth. Your elbow hard against my neck when you turned suddenly in sleep.

"What will you take?" you'd said when your eyes got heavy.

"Nothing, nothing," but when your body was still and your breaths came like the smallest even waves over your surface, I crawled out beneath the bedskirt and scooped into my hand the carcass of a fly that had beaten against the window all night and succumbed.

In the leaves of laurestine, mites build homes—or rather the leaves themselves are configured in homelike ways, the rib surrounding a dip where a mite could bury itself. Not many plants have domatia, but then not many plants fall in love.

Lonicera caprifolium, pale perfoliate honeysuckle

Some folks get freaked out by spiders, or locust swarms, but what crawls my skin is vines that send out suckers, or

FIG. 6

rootlets, or sticky hairs, or holdfasts. (Ivy, Virginia creeper, trumpet vine, cat's claw.) Twining vines, though, are perfectly polite.

"This isn't the kind that grows where you're from," my advisor says.

We're having lunch, only because he couldn't find a more intimate time to meet. He's banned me from his office hours, saying he has real students to see then. I can't tell if these punishments are calculated or if I'm paranoid (*conditioned* to paranoia). In this café too far from the Colosseum I'm racked with anxiety about who's going to pay. Racked is an exaggeration. But I do restrict myself to soup.

"If you paid closer attention," he says, sketching on his napkin a leaf with a stem puncturing the center. "See? *Japonica* and *sempervirens* don't have perfoliate top leaves."

Is he suddenly teaching me so he can prevent a lawsuit? Every time I press my research agenda, he raises objections like a gymnastics judge holding up scores. I've tried flattering him (look, I've learned how important floras can be!), impressing him (no one's done this type of urban site-specific flora in the U.S.!), lecturing him (do you understand how vital such a study would be to populations grappling with climate justice *as we speak*? How they are *stakeholders* in this data?). But he just said, "Climate justice?"

His mustache is flecked with mayonnaise.

"Didn't you get into all this," I try again, "from some sort of personal interest?"

"Personal?" His eyes tunnel back like his childhood is rushing at him, just banks and swards of poison ivy. His fat baby arms pustuled, his upper lip a balloon.

"I mean, we do what we do as adults because of the wonder we experienced as children; like, I'm sure Jacques Cousteau probably loved splashing around the tub."

"And my sandbox was filled with *Lonicera*?"

"No—I mean, maybe. Was it? But you probably liked plants always. Maybe they were an escape. Maybe your parents yelled at each other in a too-small apartment, but there was a tract of woods behind the complex where you could at least hear your own thoughts. Right? We get opened up to something, at some point, and then follow that feeling." I immediately regret the last word.

He shakes his head. "I studied."

"Plants."

"Plants," he says.

The waitress comes and leaves the check in the middle, and I say *grazie* but don't move a muscle. If he makes that expression at me one more time—that mouth-twist, brow-flick, paternal-as-f smirk—I'm going to stuff the bill in my mouth and swallow it; the scrooge didn't offer dessert.

"It doesn't seem like some shocking thing to want to do science that is also meaningful," I say, hot all over.

"If you want a story, write a memoir," he says. "You're either a botanist, in which case you study the species—the *actual* species, not the ones you *feel* are present—or you're someone who likes to keep journals."

I do NOT like to keep journals, I want to scream. I want to scream, *I DO like to keep journals, and WHAT OF IT?* The vision of a honeysuckle vine wrapping itself around his throat appears; I can't shake it.

XXXVII

Labiateae

***Lycopus*, gipsy-wort**
L. europaeus, L. exaltatus

He floats, a ghost, above the Colosseum. Death has brought him blackness, from his bloated face to his obsidian toes; in color he exalts. No, he exults. He exults in exaltation. If he could reach the wort, he'd squeeze its dye over the face of the woman, like the wanderers once did to hide their hides. He'd squeeze the woman until she popped. How's that for a story from a damned ghoul?

Salvia, sage
S. verbanica, S. clandestina

Sage, or clary, or clear-eye, was wiped beneath eyelids to catch the dust and grime of medieval life. I have trouble envisioning this, the monk or peasant swabbing at his eye with a foreign leaf, and ask Deakin if he has ever attempted to remedy himself.

He moves all the paper from one side of his desk to the other, digs a thumb into his ear, leans back, and cranes toward the window like a flower seeking sun, or a toad mimicking a flower seeking sun. A man entirely bored.

"This is the study of development, specialization, and growth."

"Yes," I say.

He moves the papers back, methodically, dismally.

I wait to hear the end of the thought, the condemnation of folktales, homespun medicine, mythology.

"Science," he says feebly.

I've pinned a spray of purple flowers to my chest, one toothed leaf still clinging. They ring around the stem like a maypole; I thrill when plants make their own design, counter to ordinary.

"Wisdom comes not through stories," he says, "but facts."

"Yes," I say, running a finger along the *Salvia*'s rib. *Rib* is a botanical term stolen from the human form. A man looked at a plant and told a story. Or a woman.

Rosmarinus officinalis, rosemary

The rosemary, for remembrance, is gone. Probably not a person alive who could say they saw it here, herbily sprouting, smelly spears lancing from the walls.

Deakin, or Lady Deakin, or whoever the f- was scribbling legends in a nineteenth-century haze, was weirdly triggered by *Rosmarinus*, not describing its use in scrumptious meals, only glancingly admitting its perfuming qualities, but instead fixating on the old tradition by which dead babies were dressed in gowns, had their cheeks ruddied, and carried ("carried") sprigs of rosemary as they were hoisted through the streets in litters on their way to the grave. *This custom is not nearly so frequent now as it used to be some years since.* Flippin' Jesus, I wonder why.

If I squint, I can almost make Deakin out, a pale little boy in a too-white gown, told to sit still in the yard while the heartier kids played European football, or with sticks. Nothing to do in that yard, in that white shift, but stare at the plants. Nothing to stir the heart but the sight of dead babies with painted faces launching down the road.

I had a different childhood; I knew nothing about plants. When something smelled good, I put it in my mouth. I still remember my tongue getting washed off by maternal hands after I bit down on the bitter resin of a rosemary branch.

Rosemary I remember.

Calminthia nepeta, lesser calamint

Two-lipped blooms. No, better: *obscurely two-lipped*.

I have never considered myself a naïve person. I have stolen rather than succumbed. And still I possessed a two-dimensional understanding of love. It was wanting, one, and giving, two. Marriage was merely a calcification of that running sap.

No, you said, marriage was a contract.

My chest caved as if punched. Contracted.

"What are you gaining?" I asked. A limb of a pollarded plane tree in your parents' yard was fat and horizontal and held us both.

"Protection from other men." You waved a leaf before your face, as if it might make you disappear.

"Feeding yourself to the lion so the tigers won't eat you."

"I'm muzzling the lion so I can pluck out its hairs, day by day, to weave a golden blanket."

I put my hand on your two lips. There was no fur.

Nepeta glechoma, ground ivy

The man with the pencil finds my sketches of Jackson's Coliseum. I've shaded the panels yellow and white, sixties-style. They look absurd in his non-Mississippi hands.

I try to describe the smell of aluminum.

"And this is a pleasant remembrance of youth?"

I must remember he's been raised in unscented boarding schools. "Childhood memories aren't pleasant," I say. "They're either important or not important."

My cotton-candy fingers glued to my dead mother's arm during the lion-taming; the feel of her hairs pulling against my skin, or my skin pulling at her hairs. Stuckness and coming-apartness.

"So why are you here?" he asks.

Here was my apartment, sprawled on a green tweed couch, my feet pressing into his thigh like cat's paws. Or *here* was the misty battleground of the relationship, which was so casual we barely knew each other's names. Or *here* was Rome, not home. All three places arguably not the right place to be.

I take the sketches out of his hands, throw them behind the couch. Whimsically, a man might think. I push my Colosseum notes toward him, as if they are masculine (good; rational; science), and the Coliseum notes are feminine (emotion; weeping; whimsy). He drags his thumb below my copy of Deakin's description—*the lips violet, spotted in the throat; anthers, before bursting, converging together into the form of a cross*—and nods. "What's this one?"

"Creeping Charlie," I say. "Alehoof, tunhoof."

He presses his palm against his temple as if I am lancing his brain.

"Field balm, gill-over-the-ground, run-away-robin."

He crawls toward me, mock-panting.

Was it my mother who sang through the clamor of the circus to the tormented lion, *Run away, Robin?*

Mentha rotundifolia, round-leaved mint

Smells of apple. Shaggy leaves, naked throat.

I cooked you a chocolate mousse with chopped leaves of apple mint, and you made a lipstick of it on your mouth. Brown with bits of green.

I made it again for the soldier because my father asked. (The roast chicken was my mother's; the brandy was his. The dessert meant as evidence of my docility.) I mixed in thyme instead.

What else might I have added? What of the myriad toxins at my fingertips? I could play Hades; I could touch my enemies and make them gray. The soldier merely squinched his lips when he ate. My father glared.

It was you I called Death. Your husband, unsuspecting Persephone. I, the mistress—the nymph Minthe. When Persephone learned of the deception, she crushed Minthe beneath her feet, made her low, made her a weed. And Hades, to temper the curse, made low Minthe so sweet-scented that none could bear to dig her out.

If I am the banished nymph, what tempering gift have you given me? I feel dead all over again, every day.

Thymus serpyllum, wild thyme

The fruit of thyme, which literally no one thinks about, is what's known as a schizocarp. I don't know what a schizocarp is (my advisor crashes his head against the desk), but I'd like to adopt the word for my own state of mind.

(*Feelings, feelings!* he screams into the wood grain.)

F- you, I scream back; *hell yeah, feelings!*

Origanum vulgare, marjoram

A priest holding a morning service at one of the altars ringing the amphitheater turns occasionally to watch my digging. I am a wayward lamb, or a messenger from the Devil. The marjoram is not for this evening's fish, to be grilled in oil and herb, but for Deakin's plate, which he will slide beneath a microscope. He has a theory about the hairs along its stem, how the cells there grow. I said I could bring samples in the morning (here I am, digging) when the hairs would be most erect, but he preferred the evening. The dark. Should I wear my armor, or is he merely lazy? I press the marjoram between thin vellum and carry it in a satchel past the women at prayer. I wink at the priest, only because I know he cannot save me.

Satureia graeca, Grecian savory

My dead mother grew savory for one year in her herb garden
(if I had a list of everything that lasted one year), and with it,
twice she cooked for us her Cajun grandmother's fricot: first
with rabbit that my father shot and swore to me was chicken,
until some drunken night when he spilled the secret to my
horrified face, and then without meat at all, because he was
too drunk to shoot. She called this second dish weasel stew,
and before I could cry, she said it was because a cook who
would sneak a meatless dish on the table was sly as a weasel.
(My brother was never lied to or teased, but then I guess he
didn't need that preparation.)

I never had fricot again. At the funeral I hoped she'd
snuck a bodiless coffin to the service. *Weasel death.*

Sideritis romana, Roman iron-wort

Plants with arrow-shaped leaves have limited common names.
Speargrass, lanceweed, ironwort. I lay them on Deakin's desk
beside the marjoram.

"If you wished to compare hairs," I say, pointing to the
Sideritis's down.

"That's merely pubescence," he says. He takes my forearm, rubs the hairs with his fingers. "This is hair." He turns
my arm over, to its nakedness. He brushes the skin with just
the lightest tips. "Pubescence. Yes?"

I make a noise of assent and return my arm to myself, wrapping it around my middle.

I wouldn't think cells could be distinguished by candle-light, but he asks me to sit beside him while he operates the microscope, all brass and black. He taps my leg with excite-ment when he spots the elongated cells, which indicate—I don't know. Another sort of woman would wish the leaves in her pocket to turn real, to become functional spears, but that sort of woman, afraid, is not the kind who would wield them.

I return home without further taps and brushes, though my skin still creeps.

Teucrium flavum, yellow germander

I'm idle one evening, sick of the green tweed couch, rico-cheting around a darker neighborhood of Rome in search of some edge of pain, aiming toward a bar where I could encounter too many drinks or just the right drunk, when I spot the man with the pencil arm in arm with a woman in a velvet coat. The order of my thoughts: *Who buys a velvet coat? Is it cold enough for that? Could I pull it off? Would it heighten my iconoclast appeal, or infantilize me? Is she the kind of woman who buys an object solely because it is pleasurable for her, and her alone, to touch?* I wanted to touch it. The touch-ing, I thought, would redeem my absurd and plummeting sense of betrayal. Because, of course, she wasn't touching it herself; *he* was touching her.

I have to give my brother credit for marrying at all, because nothing about it—the contract, the trying, the inevitable failures, the damn perfidy—is remotely appealing. But they're still at it, heartbreak aside. The other day he posted a pic of the family, each with a smile, the baby's the only one that seemed skeptical. Does he want what our father had? Do I want what my dead mother never got? Can I screw a man in Rome and not feel hurt when he screws another?

Germander is a favorite in knot gardens; long-waisted Elizabethan ladies planted it to exorcise the knots in their stomachs, hearts, brains, and ovaries. This is why depressive people paint, or schizocarps go strolling.

Prunella vulgaris, self-heal

The self-heal wears a man's collar at its neck: two leaves, stemless, that descend from the calyx into points. The bloom above is many-flowered and violet, a club of womanliness in a gentleman's shirt. With self-heal and sanicle, I want for nothing.

I wore trousers in the night for ease of climbing, but when you slowed my criminal pursuits, I felt reformed; I arrived once in a gown. You tilted your head at me, shook your unbrushed hair so that it caught in your eye, cried out—I came and fished the strands from your cornea—and said, when the involuntary tears had dried, "As a woman, you look imperfect."

Yes, and yet; yes, and yet.

Prasium majus, great hedge nettle

Basic botanical facts I know. Latin I don't.

"Endozoochory or epizoochory?" my advisor asks, waving a dried nettle like a quill, because pop quizzes are how associate professors play with graduate students. He's really trying to cover his bases.

There are five basic ways a seed gets elsewhere. It just drops off the plant (barochory), gets hurled violently outward by the plant (ballochory), gets blown away on a breeze (anemochory), floats down a stream (hydrochory), or hitches a ride on an animal (zoochory). The last category is the funnest, since you can ride on someone's back (epizoochory) or in their intestines (endozoochory), or you can be particularly attractive to ants (myrmecochory) or humans (anthropochory), or—boldest of all—you can hope your seed is eaten by an animal that's eaten by another animal that takes you so far from your native habitat that when you're shat out in Timbuktu you can colonize a whole new world (diploendozoochory).

This is how I ended up in Rome: a series of shittings.

"Epizoochory," I say.

He shakes his head.

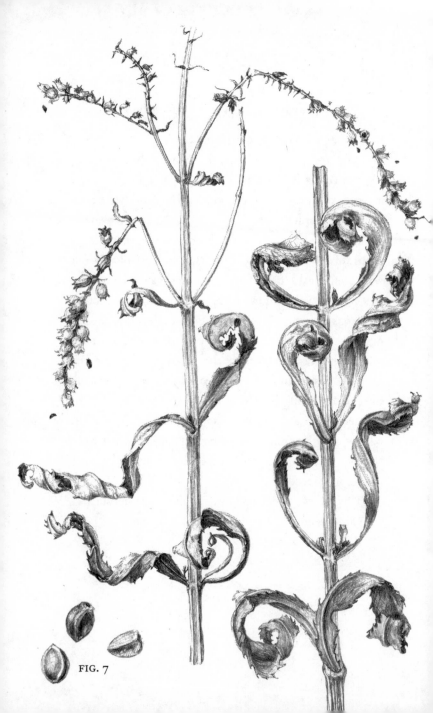

FIG. 7

Lamium vulgatum, dead nettle

Upon my death and ghostdom, I would count myself lucky to return in the guise of the dead nettle's bloom. Not blanched or hazy at all, but a ferocious pink, with a fuzzy parasol overhanging a pink trough and two wings of spotted fuchsia.

(Deakin tells me it also comes in white.)

The one nodding at me from beneath an ivy is bloody and living and loud.

("Pink," I say. "Yes," he says, "and also in white.")

It's deemed *dead* not because it kills, but because it stays inert; unlike true nettle, it cannot sting. Knowing this, do I love it less? Yes, a little.

Stachys sylvatica, hedge wound-wort

Here's my narrative for the velvet coat woman. She was browsing the racks at the outdoor market at Borghetto Flaminio, pushing past other cool kids to stroke the leather arms of jackets, when a strange man dropped a pencil at her feet. Eyes met; hearts thudded; a dinner on red-checked tablecloth was had. He said his place was a mess, so she dragged him home to her blue chintz couch and they extracted each other from their clothes, had sex with their shoes on. When she sits at her desk at the publishing house, assistant editor or young publicist, she chews on the pencil he dropped, dreaming her teeth marks dimple flesh instead.

The next time I see him, my kiss is hunting for her. This dumb sense of harm: Can I just let it go?

Wound-wort too has a schizocarp.

Ballota nigra, stinking black horehound

Ballota is Greek for rejection. A plant so fetid and foul that usually undiscriminating cows turn away in a field. Boiled and drunk, it can expel scurvy from peasants who hold their noses. Unboiled and undrunk, it bears its name with a heavy purple-flowered head. *Stinking*, yes, but why *black*? Because it is a word that further weights a doomed name? It can be spit from the mouth, the *k* aspirant, rhyming with the *k* in *stink*. Blackness hard and whiteness wide and windy. Naming carries bias, or bias worms its way to names, but we only spurn what we have not already learned to love. In darkness I found you. Black was the cloth you wore to my sister's funeral, and dark was your skin in the womb beneath your bed.

The *hore* is from *hoary*, that aged gray, not from *whore*, young and red.

XXXVIII.

Scrophularineae

Veronica, speedwell
V. beccabunga, V. chamadrys, V. officinalis, V. arvensis,
V. agrestis, V. polita, V. buxabaumii, V. hederifolia,
V. cymbalaria, V. acinifolia

Ten sweet Veronicas, blooming from the dead. One fell off and bumped its head. I called the botanist and the botanist said, "No more Veronicas, blooming from the dead."

There are only three left in the Colosseum, survivors from the ancients, species that can hold on with claws as the planet grows hotter and drier.

And there's a new one: *V. anagallis-aquatica*, which even if your Latin is as rotten as mine you can tell grows in water. What water? What are you up to, brook pimpernel? Are your wet roots heralding hope? Or are you already prepping for the floods?

Deakin writes an essay on the holy adaptability of the speedwell. How in the damp base of the Colosseum her leaves grow broad and her blooms bounteous, while higher up in the sun-washed cracks of arches, she faces tougher odds for hanging on to moisture: *the sun evaporates it—and the winds carry it away too rapidly—and the dews of night, though refreshing, penetrate not to the slender roots.* So she paces herself. The leaves are smaller, to clutch the paltry damp longer; the roots lengthen and grow tubers to store nutrients during uncertain seasons; the number of hairs on the plant multiplies, the furry army fanning out at night to trap bits of dew and folding tight against the stem during the heat of day to keep that moisture close. I have to say, I appreciate Deakin for noticing. I see you, D, for the tender way you see.

Veronica: *phérein, níkê.* She who brings victory.

Rhinanthus crista galli, yellow rattle

He floats, a ghost, above the Colosseum. The chickens are loose. *Crista* (crest), *galli* (cock), yellow coxcomb with a hollow seed that rattles. Had he a baby, a cock's chick—and he tried—he'd rattle it with this pod, wake it wailing, tickle its ear with the clang of a seed turning, a coin in the dryer, a feeling in a hard man's heart. Its mother wouldn't matter.

Euphrasia, eye-bright
E. serotina, E. lutea

A banker lived across the river in a building made of pink stone, wreaths painted, bannered, between windows, and it was from his desk I stole a pair of spectacles the autumn after I met you. He was a man I liked to watch walk. He seemed to be making adjustments to his stride each morning as he crossed my path, he on his way to his work, I on my way to the market. As if he knew walking was a performance, and he still had designs to master it. Shoulders hunched at the ears—no, down. Hips leading—no, recenter hips beneath shoulders. Head out like a duck, in like a turtle, up like a crane. I thought perhaps his glasses made him too aware.

The night I followed him home I told you I was engaged with my family. He had a sweet snoring wife, round-bellied, and two sons who began the night in two beds but suffered from nightmares; when I left with his glasses in my hand, they were flopped together, arms in a knot.

He walked more slowly in the morning, picking his way nearsighted through the crowd. Not unselfconscious, but slower. He had no second pair. By the end of two weeks, he had lost a sense of how other people moved, and his own limbs relaxed into a steady motion. One shoulder was cocked, but consistently; this was his natural state. How glad I was to have released him.

I replaced his spectacles and changed my route.

Trixago latifolia, broad-leaved trixago

Tubular magenta flowers on racemes. I wanted to be an MTV VJ so I could say things like *Tubular!* and toss my hair, and then I wanted to be a Roller Derby girl so I could wear short shorts and punch people, and then I wanted to be a war correspondent so I could tell people what was really going on while holding a gun (they don't let you hold a gun), and then I wanted to be a housewife so I could stay at home and make out with Jim McIlhenny for hours and hours, or in between whatever responsibilities he had as the office manager at the landscape company, and then I wanted to be a linguistics major so I could trace the rise and fall of popular slang (like *Tubular!*) and how coolness moves across racial and socioeconomic and regional borders, but I wasn't cool, and there was no Roller Derby team in Jackson, and the college I could afford didn't have a linguistics department, and Jim McIlhenny was only interested in making out for a couple of hours before he got tired of that.

Linaria, toad-flax
L. cymbalaria, L. vulgaris

Brideweed, bridewort, bread and butter, bunny mouths, calf's snout, dead men's bones, devil's flax, doggies, dragon bushes, eggs and bacon, eggs and butter, impudent lawyer,

Jacob's ladder, lion's mouth, monkey flower, rabbit flower, wild tobacco, yellow rod.

The pest plants are the named plants; everyone wants a term for what they see.

When young, *Linaria* yearns toward the sun, like all phototrophic plants, but after its fertilization it turns away, pushing its seed into the darkest cracks of the Colosseum, where soil has accumulated and the seed will grow.

I too claimed to be negatively phototrophic. You said *rubbish*. I pushed you in a dark corner. You unveiled your blazing face.

I want us never to have names, never to be claimed, except by the mirrors of each other, our light the only food we need.

Antirrhinum, snap-dragon
A. majus, A. orontium

It took my dead mother such f-ing effort to keep our child's garden alive: pansies for their faces, pineapple sage for smelling, snapdragons to make puppets. This was the plot I was allowed to rampage in like a litter box; the snapdragons grew rangy and wilted, the invasive *Equisetum*—horsetail, to make switches—trod into straggling submission. My brother's soccer ball cutting paths through the bed. Her tired fingers making the flowers' lips move. I never heard her arguing with my father at night about how to make room for her own dreams, but maybe I was always already asleep.

Here the snapdragons spike out of crumbling walls, jabber away in yellows and pinks and oranges, as if the secret to health is not to have children. If neglect is the trick, then, dead mother, in your absence you have saved me.

Scrophularia peregrina, nettle-leaved fig-wort

At the end of stalks, bloodred mouths open weakly. *Me*, they say. *Me*.

Deakin pays a rare visit to the Colosseum, a hat shading his white nose. He drags a cane through the dirt in the stones, nudging the roots of the creepers, the weepers, and stops at the *Scrophularia*.

"A pitiful thing," he says.

I cannot tell which of us he's addressing.

Without sitting, he pages through my notes, marks the day's sketches, clucks over a badly drawn carpel. He says I've turned too brown. He asks after my beau and doesn't listen to my report. In the pause, I watch him hear the roar of ancient crowds. Bloodthirsty.

"What will you do once the list is complete?"

"Me?" he says. He slides a finger under his hat's brim to smear the sweat. His body is both lax and coiled. "Count something else."

XXXIX.

Oleaceae

Olea europaea, olive tree

The first word for oil was *oleum*, which meant olive oil. Every subsequent use of *oil* is a derivation.

On a Croatian island there's a tree that's 1,600 years old, and women still stand on short ladders to hook the olives, which are as fresh as if newborn. This is not the oldest tree by a long shot.

Olive trees prefer poor soil. Heat. Dryness.

There are six hundred varieties of olives, or a hundred and thirty-nine, or five. Cerignola, Kalamata, Niçoise, Taggiasca, Manzanilla, Amfissa, Picholine. Brine-cured, lye-cured, dry-cured.

An olive branch insists on peace.

An oil-eater insists on virgin.

In bed I pulled the sheets over the man with the pencil's face, tucked them around our shoulders so we were encased, and in his ear softly said, trying it on for size, "I forgive you." He snorted. Grabbed for my breast and found his hand in my armpit. I kneed him in his waist. He let fly his Roman curses. I climbed on top of him in our makeshift tent and beat the back of my hand on his temple like a moth and said louder, wanting it so badly to be true, "Didn't you hear me? *I forgive you.*"

Phillyrea media, twiggy phillyrea

Mock privet, or false olive. In full growth resembling a head of broccoli, but in the cramped wilds of the Colosseum, it spreads irregularly.

The soldier asks if he can call on Deakin. He must register my shock; he lunges for my hand. Held on his knee, my fingers get squished and my palm turned over, turned over again, as he makes attempts at expression.

"I wish to explain where I'm taking you," he says.

I suggest that he's taking me nowhere at all.

He stands, forgets my hand's entrapped in his, briefly drags me down the bench. "Ah!" he says.

The promises have been made and papers signed. Deakin is not my father.

"But he has known you," he says, "in— In a particular—"

"A particular?"

"In an intimate way."

No, I want to say; *not yet, at least. I would have killed him.*

"He's offered you occupation, that is. Advanced your development. I must thank him, and explain to him his loss."

A man gaining; a man losing. A woman turned to currency.

Even kind men we can want to kill.

Ligustrum vulgare, privet

Is it a coincidence that thrushes can eat privet but men cannot? Or that the man who first cataloged the thrush family was named, sappily, Schmaltz? Or that Schmaltz died from medicating himself with the maidenhair fern? Privets make excellent topiaries. Maidens do not.

An awards dinner for scientists on a Friday night (they didn't have better plans), and my advisor is getting some expat prize, probably for worst facial hair. I show up because he uses the word *colleague* again, and I wear a vintage dress, black wool, that some woman could've worn to Vittorio De Sica's funeral. The palace's courtyard is strung with lights. Men are smoking. I slink through the crowd, feeling like James Bond. Powerful in brain and body. At the bar I see the woman from my advisor's dinner party, the one who studies tiny creatures and hoards coffee. She blows me a kiss, so I walk over.

"Sit with me for the speeches?" she says. "I'll fall asleep."

Most of what's said in the dark boozy room is in Italian,

but I understand phrases like *la bellezza della terra* and jokes about patient wives. My companion points out the men who've plagiarized or built sex dungeons in their labs.

They call out my advisor's name, and he stands up blushing, the red of his cheeks surrounding his mustache. He waits silently at the podium for a beat, establishing solemnity. It's an Oscars trick; apparently these people haven't seen the Oscars. Awed whispers echo around me.

"I want to dedicate this," he says, holding up the laminate wood plaque, "to someone special here tonight."

I glance around for anyone who would call him a friend.

"Someone who may think she'll never be in this position: honored by her peers, respected by an establishment."

Oh no.

"But I want to tell her, this could be you some day. It'll take diligence and dedication. You can't slack off on your comps."

General light laughter. My companion looks at me nervously.

"And most importantly, you'll learn that sometimes in the pursuit of knowledge, you have to take a back seat. Scientists don't arrive at projects with conclusions in mind; we're passive. Humble. Unresisting. That's how you open yourself to answers."

A murmur of assent from the crowd. My ears are liquefying. My knee is jiggling so hard under the table that the knives are dancing.

"Passive," he repeats. "What was it my old professor used to say?"

I can't wait to hear.

"'You gotta take it lying down.'" And he bellows a laugh that ricochets around the room, collecting extra laughs as it goes, men yielding to the joke, unresisting. My companion tries cutting her cloth napkin with a butter knife. "Take it lying down," he says again. And looks at me.

XL

Plantagineae

Plantago, plantain
P. major, P. lanceolatum, P. psyllium

In stories from America, I hear our great healing plant has earned a darker name: *white man's footprint*. Some black-hatted traveler carried the seed on his coat, or in the gut of his cow, and where the Puritans walked, plantain grew. Unlike more delicate weeds, it can be trampled at will. *Yes*, the natives thought, *here come the violent and the blind*.

Are you there? Has the boat taken you where white men turn their wrath from home to wilderness? Are there white-tailed deer to injure? Blackbirds to pierce? Is the whole country aflame? Are you on a boat back to me?

In the quiet of the evening, with my mother at her embroidery and me at my sketches, I feel my father's eyes on me, hunting perversion. But I wear the same dress as always, the same melancholic stare. I appear as any other woman in 1854. He thinks the insidiousness of women is our ungovernable moods. If our bodies too become unruly, then we are anarchic.

XLI.

Verbenaceae

Verbena officinalis, vervain

Also known as holy herb, for having been used to stanch
Christ's wounds. Sacrilege for the day: it's awfully spindly;
I don't know why they didn't reach for some plate-sized
sycamore leaves, or, hell, a napkin. I can just picture Jesus
wasting away, and a bunch of men dabbing at his gaping
wounds with dainty florets. (Forgive me; I swear I was raised
Catholic.)

A better legend: if thieves intentionally cut their hands
and smear vervain in the blood, they can open locks.

Do you know in all my youthful acting out, which I abso-
lutely won't blame on my dead mother, I never once pocketed
a lipstick? I had friends who sold weed, who at age twelve
bragged about sex with men three times their age, who

bound their pants legs with rubber bands so the whiskey they slipped inside wouldn't fall out. I never lifted so much as a gumball. What was it about theft that felt impossible? Bringing an object back to my house would only have thrown its emptiness into further relief.

Vervain cures everything. Unless your faith in it outpaces your stomach; high doses have been known to cause paralysis, stupor, and convulsions. These are the edges we walk across: Health, death. Comfort, risk. To harm or be harmed.

XLII.

Orobancheae

Orobanche, broom-rape
O. minor, O. ramosa

Broomrape has no leaves. It has no need of photosynthesis, but suckers to the roots of other plants to sponge out their nutrients, to ride on the wave of their chemical labors, like a cuckoo who lays her eggs in another mother's nest.

Deakin marvels at it. "What ingenuity," he says. "What evidence of God's good game." He asks me to count the broomrape's seeds. The theory is they must number in the hundreds so in scattering they might have a flea's chance of landing by a suitable root.

I wear a white apron so the seeds will stand out against the cotton. I split one capsule from the parasite, and a soil as fine as dust explodes upon my skirt. A goat steps closer to investigate; I kick at his tufted heels. I smooth the dust around into groups—a group of roughly ten, no wider than a whorl on my fingerprint; a group of fifty; one hundred. I am a scientist, which means I do not count them all. Eleven hundred seeds, I estimate, then stand and brush the filth from my dress. The goat has folded its legs for a nap. I bend the stem and count capsule by capsule, sixty-six in all. I write the total number in my notebook—72,600 seeds—and consider what to share with Deakin. The whole number, or half, or to tell him the capsules were empty, and parasites born are parasites raised. I have seen them in a field of sunflowers, rising brown and fungus-like, sticks of naked flesh, as the *Helianthus* heads nod down, sucked dry.

And yet this *rape* does not derive from *rape*, but *rapum*—turnip.

XLIII.

Acanthaceae

Acanthus mollis, smooth bear's-breech

A large waxy-leaved plant so striking a Greek sculptor wove it into his capitals, and from then on Corinthian was a style, the tip-top of any column top.

I sometimes think the man with the pencil should be an architect, the way he draws boxes around the rooms of his life. It's okay, he says, that he sometimes sees another woman, women, and I am free too, we all are free, freedom is the catchword of the twenty-first century. I nod and don't say *I want to be built in*, but I do, I very much want to be built into a structure so that no one can remove me without the roof falling in.

Maybe I've been making the walls all my life. The risk,

of course, is it might be only big enough for one. But if the man with his eraserless pencil won't help me—if my advisor won't, if my father, my brother, my childhood gynecologist—I give myself permission to self-construct.

XLIV.

Boragineae

Echium, viper's bugloss
E. vulgare, E. italicum

Spikes of violent blue, split-tongued styles, blue pollen. (Blue pollen!) Bugloss the term for a tongue.

Deakin met my suitor, and all the men approved. Bargains made in speech that carry over into beds. My mother, opium-dizzy, wants to make a dress. I tell her I have dresses, that one more cannot make a difference in God's eyes. She drops her chin onto her chest, runs her thumb along her pouch of needles. I should fall to my knees and beg for a dress. She needs something to do. Once I have a dress, once the dress is wed, will I become a woman who needs something to do?

I'll have a daughter, and I'll tell her out there in the world is another woman, a *you*, and though she too wore her dress and wed, we briefly were something louder, something in motion, something two-tongued.

Cerinthe aspera, rough-leaved honeywort

The leaves taste of *new wax*, one herbalist wrote. Old men crouched down chewing leaves: this is a dream I have when I'm extra lonely and feel like I might dry up into a wind-blown wisp. I never thought I'd miss home.

"Christmas?" my brother texts, impervious to rebuffs.

Yes, I want to say. *Come get me.*

Does making my own path mean asking for help, or not needing it?

Heliotropium europaeum, European turnsole

You pushed me down behind a stand of summer tomatoes, the sellers in their skirts masking us, and pointed: *There*. I watched all the men walking. They turned their bodies away from the vegetables, their eyes holding level above the barkers' wrapped heads. Who would want one of them? Their arms held close, their bodies defended from female space.

There, you said again.

The man in the tall black hat? The red cravat? The striped vest? With the brown wool pants, or the gold-chained watch, or the cane, or the rag, or the pipe, or the cards?

Beside the tomatoes a woman sold white sprays of turnsole from a bucket. They nodded when each man passed. I couldn't see which was yours.

Lithospermum, gromwell
L. arvensis, L. purpureo-caeruleum

Purpurocaeruleum means "purple! blue!" This is how my heart goes too.

I totally flower first in a kind of reddish-violet: oh yes—him, him—give me more of that—him all the time, nesting in my head in any moment of space (driving, falling asleep, listening to my advisor threaten me). And then inevitably my flower turns blue: oh I don't know—him is not what I imagined—sometimes him—his skin, but not his speech, not the way he doesn't ask me how I'm human, and all my thinking now is *maybe, maybe, how do you know*.

You don't know.

These are my advisor's words as he points me to the chemicals that cause change in the color of an inflorescence. There are some things knowable—anthocyanins, carotenoids—that are simply unknown by me.

"You don't know," he says when I ask. Not *we don't know*.

My body feels purple with rage, and turning bluer every day. My body's an f-ing ball of fury.

Symphytum tuberosum, tuberous-rooted comfrey

You wore a comfrey-colored dress to the theater, a matching cream ribbon around your head. I with my father and mother, you with yours. The men around us like the water around fishes.

At intermission between acts of weeping women and corsairs, you stumbled on the stairs and dropped a note. A few steps later, I shuffled it under my shoe. In the powder room, I sat before a mirror and unfolded the paper.

It wasn't an intentional stumble, a ploy.

You'd twisted your ankle. The note wasn't for me.

Your future husband had written your name across the top, all its loops cramped in his inelegant hand, and asked for an assignation. He'd caught your comfrey-colored dress too, and read it not as my sun but his.

They wrapped your ankle in its leaves (common name knitbone); my heart too waited for a poultice. *Sundown*, he'd written. But night was mine.

Borago officinalis, borage

"I'm not leaving until you tell me how to get funds," I don't say.

"What are your plans next summer?" he does say. Meaningless jazz plays in the background; people I don't know tink glasses in his kitchen. He's spread wide in a blue velvet chair. Has he ever brought a male assistant home? Should I have checked on this before showing up to his posh apartment at night for a "gathering"?

"Mississippi," I remind him.

Borage causes forgetfulness when mixed with wine. (That's the least of what I'd mix in that man's wine.)

The record player spins soundlessly on the end of an LP. The sound, rather, is native: metal on vinyl. *Scritch, rub, scritch, rub.* The cheese plate looks as if a mastodon has stampeded through it. The mastodon was my mouth. I'm a graduate student, not a lady in a novel.

Two other young botanists, Italian, are standing in the small hallway by the door, saying sweet things to each other in rhyming syllables.

"Let me know, of course, how I can continue to be of help."

Continue to?

"Tell me how the f- to get funds," I don't say again.

"Whatever you need," he says, and with the tip of one shoe kicks off the other. Leather.

Star-shaped blue flowers—not pure blue but bruised, as if the flower could never, not ever, get what it wanted, but only what hurt.

Myosotis arvensis, field-scorpion grass

Deakin in his dressing gown, his mother with her needle-work loose in her lap, her capped head nodding to one side. By firelight I write down his narration.

"A forget-me-not," he says. "The limb of the corolla as long as its tube."

I scribble. "Culinary uses?"

"Call it an emblem of affection."

"Shall you not tell the story of its name?"

He ties the belt of his gown tighter; his mother jerks out a snore. "I imagine," he says, "that a groom gave it to his bride for her wedding spray, a testament to God's bindings."

I think of its yellow eyes in the field of blue.

When I was young I had a book of painted flowers, bright plates between pages of poems I couldn't read, and there was buried the real tale of love, the yellow-eyed version. "Two lovers were strolling along the Rhine," I say, "and the woman saw a flower she desperately wanted. So the man reached for it, but in reaching he fell into the river."

"Where did you read this?"

"And as he went under, the stem in his hand, he cried out, *Vergiß mich nicht!* And drowned."

Deakin throws a receipt into the fire, turning it briefly green. "Readers of a flora don't want tragedy," he says.

"Botany *is* tragedy," I say.

Cynoglossum pictum, Madeira hound's tongue

So named because there was a dog on Madeira (what is Madeira? An island? Why do all islands begin with M? Malta, Mauritius, the Maldives, Mallorca, Mykonos, Madagascar, Martinique) who found herself starved—starved because some explorer had dumped her and a crate of puppies and returned to the mainland with a satchel of saffron, or whatever was mined on islands. And the starved dog had tried her hand at eating every single thing between one sea and the other: grass, shrubs, bees, mice. It was only when she tasted puppy, her own flesh, that her tongue turned *flesh-coloured, marked with darker veins, the scales in the mouth . . . pink or red*. The only thing that satisfies is the self.

I'm inspired to dig deeper now that Deakin's stories have turned dark; I read his entry on the forget-me-not with a happy horror. Drowning German lovers? How did that make it into print?

An Englishwoman stops to ask, kindly, what I'm doing (why my face looks so devilish), and I show her my notes with a smile.

"I'm telling stories about flowers," I say.

She nods, understanding. "They named me Daisy." *That's a story*, she means. She puts her earbuds back in.

Anchusa italica, Italian alkanel

Covered in bristles—spines of roughened hair, barbs re-curved, prickles that blanket the soft parts; this is why I haven't been touched.

I thought I saw him that time, a hat leaving your house with a begonia in his lapel, but he was just a man from the bank, a man about money, a man shuffling contracts. Who looks at all the flowers in the world and chooses begonia?

I make a new pact, and it's with neither you nor the soldier, and in its terms I demand new purpose. I'll write my own flora: a kind of progeny.

XLV

Primulaceae

Anagallis, pimpernel
A. arvensis, A. caerulea

He floats, a ghost, above the Colosseum. The poor man's weatherglass, at the first sign of love or thunder, tightens its thighs, binds up the seed. He writhes, thinking of the thighs. Were he to drink of scarlet pimpernel, to pimple well, to break into boils, to choke, to heave, to slick his teeth with froth, to stand betrayed—O pimpernel, point your vane at the girl who clouded her mind with murder.

Cyclamen, cyclamen
C. hederifolium, *C. europaeum*

My dead mother planted a clutch of cyclamen on the far side of a grandfather oak behind our house—she put them where she hoped I wouldn't find them. (She's dead; I can't ask her to confirm or deny.) But she must've seen the wreck of my child's garden and thought, *I must save something for myself.* If I ever turn into a mom, I'd hide everything I own in secret stashes (potato chips, nice spoons, lace undies, first editions, dark chocolate), so I'm not blaming her, I'm only noting. The cyclamen, *sow bread* to the Italians, were too fine for my mayhem.

I found them when I ran away, my cotton panties in a plastic lunch box, next to toothbrush, comic, Barbie. I hid behind that oak for three hours, longer than I'd ever done anything in my life, and stuck my pinky into the cyclamen's throats.

A child doesn't need trauma to make her run away, but trauma doesn't hurt.

I didn't stay long enough to watch the upside-down petals die back, the trumpets turn bare, the nude stem start curling autumnward, tightening against the earth. Someone found me.

Wild hogs feast on cyclamen's hideous tubers; they dig up and dizzy themselves on the UFO corm and its jellyfish roots. Their hooves stamp out the heart-shaped leaves, and the flowers are neither here nor there. The rest of the plant is used by humans: to drive out ringworm, to stun a school of fish, to flush out a fetus. (So much fetus-flushing in a flora; you'd think all medieval women had to do was walk into the woods and start chowing down.)

I never went back to visit the cyclamen. I knew enough by then to know what a secret was.

XLVI.

Convolvulaceae

Convolvulus, bindweed
C. arvensis, *C. sepium*

Like morning glory, like moonflower, like evening primrose
on a vine. One of the most smothering weeds on the con-
tinent, with seeds that can lie in wait in barren soil for fifty
years, or until the rains.

I was raised with the belief that beauty was never ineradicable. That beauty's merit was in transience and its inevitable
fade. As a girl I opened my blooming face to the world, for
a window. My cheeks lack color. My seeds are drying. I was
seeking, you joked, the wrong pollinator. But you too only
saw me in youth; you left before I began to wilt.

When I see bindweed clawing the altars in the Colosseum, I cast a prayer that they might stay. *Be good*, I think.
Be long beautiful.

XLVII.

Solaneae

Hyoscyamus albus, white henbane

A black-throated narcotic. Did I hurl this epithet at the henbane (which, what the f-, isn't here anymore; not even bane I guess can stand the twenty-first-century furnace) or at my lover, ex-, the man with the f-ing pencil, who wrote me a letter and left it under a seat in the Colosseum, marked with a cairn of stones so any fool could've found it, in which he confessed some f-ed-up eighteenth-century confusions, on the order of Myth and Self and the Sublime, so that I had to skip ahead to the end of the note to learn what he meant to do with my heart, which was *stay in touch, kid*.

In touch. Touch-me-not. *Noli me tangere*. Which of us Jesus, which of us Mary Magdalene. The gap between two

FIG. 8

hands, between one body and another, holds all the sorrow and freedom in the world.

Verbascum, mullein
V. sinuatum, V. blattaria

For use in killing cockroaches.

Solanum, nightshade
S. dulcamara, S. nigrum, S. villosum

I went home with the note in a twist in my damp hand and crawled under the bed, me and the paper and a pillow and, hours later, a bottle of bourbon, brought from the South via checked bag. Words and liquor and dark. I'm starting to conflate men; in order to stay sane I have to be careful where I direct my fury.

(My forgiveness had obviously been a joke.)

I thank the god of the Catholics that not once in my ravage of a life have I wanted to pull the darkness up over myself. I am an implementer. I aim the darkness out.

XLVIII.

Gentianeae

Chlora perfoliata, perfoliated yellow-wort

I sidestep the yellow-wort, nod at its nodding heads, which, like pimpernel, expand in sun and curve into themselves when clouds arrive. Feminine little flowers, with their penetrated leaves, punctured hearts, perfoliate.

Deakin is rushing the reports, sure that the wedding will steal his amanuensis, not understanding, of course, that all along I've been stealing the flora from him. I'm asked to come to him each night, papers in hand. He knows not what else I've kept in my pockets: baubles, knives, seeds.

Erythraea, centaury
E. centaurium, E. lutea

A candelabra can hold either pink star-shaped flowers or candles. The term, my advisor tells me, is corymbose panicle.

"Or candelabra," I say.

A storm outside has turned the afternoon to night, and he lights a single lamp on his desk, the green-caped kind. I'm here to make one more pitch for funding. One last by-the-book attempt.

"Tea?" he asks.

I have a photocopy of Deakin because the first edition in the office has a crumbly spine that smells of graves, and my advisor won't let me touch it. So the papers fold open on my lap like cranes. *The whole plant is without odour*, I read, *but is strongly impregnated with a bitter resinous matter.*

"Like some women I know," he laughs.

"Centaurs," I say, "were invented so nymphs wouldn't have to look at the bottom half of a man."

He leans onto his arms, onto his desk, his top half lunging forward under the green light. "I'd swear you were a woman who knows what she wants."

I lean too, toward his face against the backdrop of a thousand points of rain, the window breaking each one. In my pocket is an imaginary gun.

XLIX

Ericaceae

Arbutus unedo, strawberry-tree

Under the branches of a strawberry tree we sit—not the one twenty feet tall growing out of the once-soil of the Colosseum, as if a martyr's blood had sprouted it, had manifested once more in the small ruby fruits, but one in the Villa Borghese, tamed, untainted by Christ.

"The *tricolore* of the nation," the soldier says. The green leaves, the red berries, the spring-white blooms that now are gone.

"Or hope," I say, "and faith," I say, "and love."

"A speech for a wedding," he says, and takes my hand, blue-gloved, in his.

Pliny was the one who named it, *unedo*, in his fussiness.

Unum tantum edo, I eat only one. I can't tell the soldier this, for he would turn it romantic, and its romanticism isn't his.

I eat only one, and it was you.

Erica arborea, tree-heath

My father had a briarroot pipe he was given after the death of my dead mother, as if by adopting a new bad habit he could erase his old one (if love is a bad habit, which yes it is), or maybe the intent was more contemplative: that in staring at the rising smoke he could meditate on how wispy our own lives are. Could imagine my dead mother rising in a vapor to heaven.

You have to wait fifty years to harvest the burls of *E. arborea*, cut the great knots out of the trunk, cook them, dry them, carve them, pack them with tobacco, hand them to a grieving man, watch them soothe him into sleep.

But you could pack a pipe with other things.

L

Amaranthaceae

Amaranthus, amaranth
A. blitum, A. retroflexum

The morning after the soldier touched my neck beneath the strawberry tree, a letter waits on the table by the door, between my father's hat and my mother's umbrella, white, blazing white, like a magnolia on the wood.

I have gone a hundred days without you. I have written a hundred letters. I have dreamed three times as many dreams, my mind running fast through all the scenes of you: on a boat, alone, swimming, wet-haired, with me, an orange in your mouth, hatted, with your husband, rolling down a stocking slow, weeping, your cheek against my foot, under clouds, elbows on a bridge, his hand against your ear, in front of art, behind a mob, with a rose-cheeked stranger, cold, a dew of sweat on your lip.

I take the letter upstairs. My father calls after me. The soldier is coming again tonight, someone make a rum cake. I only know the recipe because I once took a cake from the barber's oven, left overnight to cool, and out of not shame but mischief I made another to put in its place before dawn: a whole thieving night spent baking. I hid below the windows to watch his wife cut it in the morning, the twist of their tongues as they felt for the gap between what had been (cherry) and what was (rum). *But—* they said. *Did you—?* they said. *The cherries must have—* and the answer was *gone bad.* But I knew from how I made it that mine was the better. They each ate double. The liquor on their lips I could smell from behind glass.

I drag the letter beneath the bed, put it first in my mouth to see if I can hunt you out, then lie against it, crisping its folds. Its sheets nothing like our sheets. I cannot seem to take in air all the way, but it lies shallow in my throat. You used to press my back and say, *In the morning it will be another day.* I have been waiting a hundred days to hear, have been writing the names of plants instead, have been telling myself flower stories, waiting for nature to reinstate her order, in which a thing germinates, grows, flowers, fruits, and dies. A bird may come, or a moth in the night, but a thing is a thing whether or not a bird comes, or a moth in the night.

This will either say *I'm sorry I'm sorry* or else *god help me this is my last, I cannot, bloody hell, not without your touch, the ocean take my body* or else *the water's fine, the view lovely, he's a darling, wish you were here.*

An amaranth fruit, green and indistinct, hides within it a black seed, the size of a single breath.

Santalaceae

Osyris alba, white poet's cassia

"Haustoria are roots that grow from one plant into another," he says, the storm traveling west now, thunder at a distance.

"Symbiosis," I say. In my backpack is an application for funding for next summer (American Philosophical Society's Lewis and Clark Fund for Exploration and Field Research), two references required. One letter's coming from an ecology professor, but the second needs to be from—

"Parasitism," he says.

"I guess that's why they call it 'white poet.'"

He's a man who doesn't believe in symbiosis. They have a word for this in the botanical field, for people who can't honestly believe that equality exists in nature, for men who've never been loved, or never had a dream, or were told in high school to stop looking at Becky, you're creeping her out: the word is cranks.

He once told me, quoting a lecture from some scientific society at UNC four score years before he was born, "There are no 'cranks' in the ranks of botany!" I thought he was joking, so I found the original text, and what the f-, he was right. And it gets worse. Not only does the *wholesome restraint which the habitual exercise of the observing faculty . . . places upon the imagination* help control *its vagrant wanderings*, but *[i]t guards also against misuse of the too often "fatal gift of expression,"* you know, that gift *which so frequently makes its possessor mistake words for things.*

I pull out the manila folder with the eight-page proposal titled *Flora Colisea Mississippiana*. He smiles, puts his cheek in his hand to soften his face, a hunter setting himself as bait. Soon the rain will pass and all that will be left is dark.

"Tell me what you want," he says, wholly serious, still laughing at me—so f-ing loud—with his eyes. No one ever told me expression could be fatal.

LII.

Euphorbiaceae

Euphorbia, spurge
E. peplis, E. chamaesyce, E. helioscopia, E. exigua

He floats, a ghost, above the Colosseum. The girls have left, tending other needs at night. No one is left to drink the spurge, called madwoman's milk. As if daisies had mouths for milk. No, they fondle other teats, they make treats of emetics, they lace drinks with powdered root. Did he taste madness when he sipped? What filled his stomach when his stomach set on fire?

Mercurialis, mercury
M. perennis, *M. annua*

Dog's mercury grows in shade. Alkaline soil. Simple leaves, ovate. Made for dogs.

In the Colosseum it hides from innocents—the laundress's sheep, the priest's daughter. It calls my name. I have found in my career that objects have wishes, and a thing desirous of being stolen will call your name. Its voice like yours, but bluer. (The plant turns blue as it dries.)

Twelve leaves in my pocket. Is that enough? Twenty-four.

After I read your letter I went to Deakin's house, crying out in pain, and was given more. I was almost given too much pain. It is not your fault.

I once tried to tell you, in a night garden, what plants would make you ill—not to tempt you but so in our fantasy of all the buildings fallen to dust and the humans melted into water you would know what to feed me in our bower. *With no rooms*, you said, *what would you steal?*

Dog's mercury smells of spoiled fish, tastes of nothing, sears the lining of the stomach. First a hemorrhage, unseen, then a swelling of the jaw, slow spasms in the muscles, lethargy, sleep. (The victim turns blue as he dies.)

LIII.

Polygoneae

Rumex, dock
R. pulcher, R. acetosella

I think Deakin's getting lonelier. Listen to these adjectives: *flowers, few, in rather distant whorls, drooping, on short stalks.*

I, on the other hand, am not few. I'm newly manless, sure, unless you count my advisor, who said he'd consider writing a recommendation, dangling that *maybe* like something lewd; or the old man in the apartment above mine who only owns dressing gowns; or the window washer on Via Veneto who drops pieces of his lunch when I walk by, as if he could mark me with crumbs; or my own father, who once a week sends an email reporting on the state of the bird feeder ("third jay seems dominant on Supreme Blend"). But I feel like each day I multiply.

Is it because I know more words? *Am* knowing more words?

(My grant proposal was really f-ing good, that's why.)

Polygonum, persicaria
P. persicaria, P. mite, P. aviculare, P. dumetorum

If applied to skin, knotweed is known to stunt growth.

I hide the mercury leaves in the pouch my mother made, blue-ribboned, to cross my waist beneath my wedding dress. One week now. Skin then silk and leaf and lace.

One week and I will be a wife; once wifed, I will stop writing to you.

LIV.

Urticaceae

Parietaria officinalis, pellitory of the wall

I don't know which is nicer, flattery or flagellation. He's on his knees again, in the dust, his head under my hand—this is how we met, reversed. He's saying all the right things. I'm not denying there's an urge to squeeze his temples until they smash, to juice his brain as he runs through his excuses. Youth, he says. A difficult mother. Feelings as distant as a ship from a lighthouse. "What the f-?" I say. "Are you the ship or the lighthouse? Who's the rocks?" He moves on.

Been trying his whole life to get over something. ("Over what?") Too busy running. ("Is this a country song?") Scared, he was scared to go all the way to the bottom of his heart. ("What's down there, an f-ing kraken?")

But he did. He went. And I was there.

It's the hay of his hair that does me in. That I can touch a body that isn't mine, with permission. How does God not come every night and stroke the arms of us all?

The stamens of the pellitory curve over the pistil, protective, but when the plant is brushed, the stamens shoot back and spray pollen like a firehose. (As Deakin notes, perhaps himself becoming more sexually assertive, this party trick is *best observed on a hot summer's day, when they are easily excited into action by the least movement.*)

He picks up pouches of dust and spreads them on my bare toes. I have a lock of his hair between thumb and finger and could pull at any moment.

"I want to be scared by you," he says.

How come vulnerability only looks good on men? I tell myself I'm not scared of anything.

Stacks of dried pellitory, rich in niter, have been known to spontaneously ignite. I take him home.

Urtica, nettle
U. pilulifera, U. urens, U. dioica, U. membranacea

The bouquet of nettles on the table, between the candles and the butter dish, alarms my father. (*What will he think!*) They spray their serrated leaves like battle wounds. The structure of the thorn, invisible from the dining chair, is the same as a viper's fang, with pressure on the curve causing the venom to travel. I've mixed dock in the arrangement, an instant salve should someone hurt themselves. And my intent is not to injure. The two plants, poison and cure, grow where humans have left buildings to ruin. They are ghosts of us, our two halves, sprung out of disturbance and abandon.

(I have been abandoned.)

I put the nettle in a vase the way a girl would hang a mirror above a basin.

Ulmus campestris, small-leaved elm

Would you believe there's still an elm in the Colosseum? A sapling, old enough to manifest that strange winged bark, sturdy enough to hold me as the man I forgave presses me into it, his hands pulling at my hips.

This was one of the first trees I learned, so nicely distinguishable. The bark, the seeds like paper coins, the asymmetrical leaves, one half stretching longer than the other at the base, as if to prove something.

He turns me into a tree only because I allow it. It's okay sometimes—I think—to want a man's want. To have a hurt, and let it go. I've spent so much energy on suspicion. Tonight before or after sex I'll text my brother and tell him I'm sorry, that I feel for him and her, and all I can do is listen and hope they find a way toward happiness. Hurting just comes with the territory.

Ficus carica, fig-tree

Strange that we should call leaves heart-shaped, rather than admitting so many hearts are leaf-shaped. Figs for dessert, vulva-shaped. (Not a fruit, but an infructescence.) No wonder fig leaves must cover it.

The soldier blanches, my father pulls his hair, my mother floats on a cloud of opium. "The flowers, dear, delightful."

The bench in the front hall across from the table where the letter was is where we sit. I stare at the table, letterless; he stares at my hand. My mind is numb with what Deakin has done: an act I can't yet speak. The soldier taps on my fingers like a harpsichord. I wait for him under lamplight to protest my coldness, to take a stand for kind behavior, to force a kiss or cancel the wedding. Seven days left, and my nerves are tight.

Livia smeared a fig with poison (what kind?) to kill Augustus.

"I'm sorry," he says.

I hide my hands under my skirt so he can't keep tapping.

"I don't know why," he says, "but I find myself feeling terribly sorry. You must tell me if I'm the cause of your paleness, if you can't grow an affection for me. I can't bear—"

"No," I say, needing friendship.

"Do I hurt you?"

"No," I say. Without my hands, I must press my eye against my shoulder to stop the water.

LV

Ambrosiaceae

Xanthium, burweed
X. spinosum, X. strumarium

Cocklebur seeds float. In the monsoons that drowned the countryside near Sylhet in Bangladesh, the rain washed all the food away. (Can I imagine that world? Where one morning my food is gone, my home, a child too small to swim? Increasingly, yes; the waters and the fires, as they kill us, make a single globe of us.) Their stomachs were all dried out, so the people gorged themselves on what floated: cockleburs. Nineteen people died. Before they did, the toxicologists tell us, they suffered from *altered mental status*. What was the alteration? Were they giddy? Did they see dinosaurs tall as temples? Were their hands turning into leaves? The mean victim was female, age sixteen. Old enough to have her brain already altered.

LVI.

Chenopodiaceae

Chenopodium, goose-foot
C. polyspermum, C. ambrosioides, C. vulvaria,
C. album, C. muralis, C. hybridum

This is what men think of me: a stem covered in a *greasy, pulverulent, foetid substance*, stinking of fish left out too long, *an extremely nauseous odour*, called *C. vulvaria*. I am not the one who gets to name. The goosefoot hides in shadow behind the Altar of Mary Magdalene, and I pluck her and wear her in my breast. She smells of nothing I know.

I doze beneath my sun hat, sitting up, arms around my knees. I wish I could wait for another letter to tell me you were wrong, so my blood can go on pumping. We are nothing, you and I, stinking poisonous sluts, pinned with Latin words.

I leave the Colosseum through the ancient exitways, the vomitoria.

Atriplex patula, spreading halbert-leaved brache

We're really in the weeds now, things without even a nice color to make them worth someone's attention. This is where, if I'm being honest, I would've stopped making notes. ("But it has a rhomboidal perianth!" my advisor says. "So does your mom!" I reply.)

In my bed the man I forgave sleeps with his arms as wide as Christ's. I piano my fingers up and down his chest and try to remember he was a boy once, and still has that sweet heart. I don't think we won't leave each other again, but we eat eggs in the mornings and I learned he doesn't like loud noises, or his uncle, and when I yell about science he listens. He bought me peanut butter at an international grocery because I said I was homesick.

A row of dried stems lines the sill beside my sink, next to the coffee cups. Today, at least, I think it's all right not to feel pain.

LVII.

Phytolaccaceae

Phytolacca decandra, Virginian poke

I write you a response in pokeberry. My love, my love, you won't see it. With the berries in a bowl, how tempting to gorge myself on their poisonous ink—but my suffering cannot grow larger than it is. I shall start with your tone: *I'm so pleased!* The purple ink bleeds from the tail of the exclamation; the page is overrun by worms. I repeat: *Your adventures marvelous! My apprenticeship illuminating!* I write all the names of men I know; I'm only matching you. *He he he he he.* How can a body change? If her soil does. Her climate. The heat turned dry, the mistrals damp.

The poke comes from southern America, where humans chain other humans to prevent change. How it found its way to the Colosseum is a story of any migrant, of the seeds that dropped off the fur of lions who ate Christians, so that God could mix His peoples in a single bowl.

Purple berries with black blood. You once whispered we could move to those States and begin a righteous slaughter, a redemption. (You thought I was a criminal.) But whiteness isn't truth, it's ghostliness. Already the ink is fading. Poor man's indigo.

I spent one hundred hours today imagining your body. It said all the right things.

Six days left to marriage. I still plot my revenge.

LVIII.

Orchideae

Orchis, orchis
O. pyramidalis, O. papilionacea

To clarify, *Orchis* has a spurred lower lip; *Ophrys*'s is un-spurred. One of them got kissed too much.

My advisor has asked me to describe, in words, the structure of an orchid blossom. This is a test to determine whether I'll get a letter of reference out of him. (Not the only test, I bet.) Since there aren't any orchids here anymore—beauty not sturdy enough for a climatological apocalypse—I look at the pictures on the internet, pornographic. "Striated lower lip," I write. "Three top horns. Awns? Cluster of three to five flowers per inflorescence, fuchsia. Small throat. Achingly small. Almost voiceless."

FIG. 9

I hand in my notes with a sketch of a woman, legs spread like wings. (I'll never forgive him for reading my journal.)

"Is this supposed to be an orchid?" he asks.

"Oh, sorry!" I say, pointing to the bend in her knee. "It's a grasshopper. I'm also studying entomology."

Ophrys arinifera, early spider orchis

We each are allowed a single fundamental lie: either it was your letter, or it was you. (*Change*, I hear you say again; *what about change.*)

This orchid carries its lie in its swollen lower lip, velvet-brown with an H marked in blue. Deakin calls it sexually deceptive. It manufactures the scent of female mining bees (who, when the flowers bloom in May, are still asleep in hibernation), so the gentlemen will hunt them out, fall upon the orchid lips, and, after spending themselves, will fly away in a coat of pollen. In warmer summers, the ladies emerge too soon and the orchid is left unsatisfied; in a generation of warm summers, the orchid might fade to nothing.

Did you seduce me to survive?

LIX.

Irideae

Crocus minimus, least purple crocus

A deer used to dig my dead mother's crocuses out of the January soil and snack on the bulbs like apples. I remember her with an upside-down broom, spilling profanities. (She gave me my tongue.)

What I said in the proposal that my advisor will never read is that my dead mother believed that plants meant something. Not just in the doctrine-of-signatures way, or the yellow-rose-for-friendship way. She believed life was a gray wash, humans climbed it with their fingernails, and the only interruption, the only proof of beauty, was a piece of living green pushing through a coffin of spring soil.

It matters what. I thought it didn't—that a flora was a

fealty exercise for grad students, like cleaning baseboards—but each thing is its own thing, and it matters what.

My dead mother built a wire-fence house over the last crocus bulb, and when it finally bloomed—not purple but a surprising white—she hunched over the tiny cup for half an hour, breathing, and then took the fence away and put a knife and fork beside it. In the morning the meal was over. Without the thirty crocus minutes, her life would've been thirty minutes shorter.

I want, now, to say what matters.

Triconema columna, Columna's trichonema

Yellow-throated blue flowers, hanging like earrings on six-inch scapes.

My mother sleepily gives me sapphires, *something blue*.

In my armoire is a hatbox stuffed with stolen jewels, *something untrue*. I have a salmon satin gown from a woman who eloped; a cutting of double-flowered oleander from a duke's inner courtyard; a button; a knife; and you. Not you.

In the silk pocket beneath my hanging white dress the mercury leaves are almost dried. Five days left.

LX.

Amaryllideae

Narcissus poeticus, narcissus of the poets

Narcissi, the fairest among them all, / Who gaze on their eyes in the stream's recess, / Till they die of their own dear loveliness. It's Deakin quoting Shelley here—Deakin, whose heart seems to be coming out of his chest in strings of taffy. Tell me, tell me, who did you wrong, old botanist?

Is it a twenty-first-century conceit that *you are enough*? Did no one in your self-help circuits whisper that to you back then? Were you told looking in the mirror was a sin? Was I told wrongly that I'm more important than my neighbor? Were you too somebody's dead mother, Deakin?

Liliaceae

Muscaria, grape hyacinth
M. racemosum, M. comosum

The smell of wet starch. Of clotheslines, drying sheets. That no one has taken them in before dark suggests a woman is absent. I perch on his windowsill in my robber's pants and judge his undressing. His belly bulbous with ham and wine. He is not large but misshapen—composed of his consumptions. I blink away the memory of his body. (How I wanted to run to you that night and be washed clean!) My bile rises. On his desk the papers of science have been shuffled like cards, as if a genus of plants was a hand to play. He snuffs the candle with wet fingers. Someone has left on his mantel a bouquet in a green jade vase. Little purple urns (others call them bells) that catch the ashes of the moon. It being autumn, they must be made of marble. A marble muscari, scentless, though no remembrance of a woman is without smell. In the field, they would reek of wet starch.

Allium, garlic
A. ampeloprasum, A. vineale, A. roseum, A. subhirsuta, A. album

Wild onions grew in unmowed Mississippi lawns when I was young enough to put the umbels in my mouth. You think it's just the memories that we lose, but the fireflies started fading, then the roly-polies, the wild honeysuckle, the onions. The land shifts slow, then fast, so the pictures we draw for ourselves are like cartoons of a dead place.

Write it down before it's gone. (This isn't what Deakin thought, or really any pre-industrialist, who listed because listing was fun, a catalog of wonders, a test of how much a human could know. Plants didn't change, only our understanding of them.)

The tourists in their Tevas don't smell the alliums because they're tuning in to something else: history, stone, absence. They want white things, blank things. But corpses smell, and onions. The wild leek, its leaves sagging at the other end of the year, can hold five hundred flowers in its papery cap. More flowers on a single stalk than Deakin counted species. More humans here than there is air to breathe.

Onions make you cry not because of the lachrymatory

factor or the syn-propanethial-S-oxide, but because when you see them you remember everything you've lost since the day you were born, squalling and raisined, and someone handed you a map of the universe, every star and seed with a name. You don't know it anymore. Write it down before it's gone.

Ornithogalum, star of Bethlehem
O. umbellatum, O. narbonense

Its Biblical name not *star of Bethlehem* but, in fact, *dove's dung*. I wonder if another woman on this windowsill would see the scientist inside as something shining. *Leaves, radical, numerous, linear, flaccid, soon withering.*

The night I received your letter—all those days ago—I took my tears to Deakin and his mother (asleep) and said, "I can't." I blame myself for not knowing the rest of the words to speak. Away with you went everything else of meaning: the eating of toast at breakfast, the lacing of my chemise, the breathing of air, the dutiful recording of species. I could still marry. Resignation, in fact, was all I could do, so I came to tell him, "I can't." He read my red eyes different.

Asphodelus fistulosus, onion-leaved asphodel

"So what did he say?" asks the man I forgave, his mouth chipmunked with burrata.

I found a receipt for flowers in the tote of groceries he carried up to my apartment, but I only got cheese and pole beans; the flowers must've gone to someone prettier, newer, more reluctant. I don't mind—it's my life he's revolving around, not the reverse. (I'm trying to convince myself of my own centrality; be patient.)

"Advisors don't *say* anything. They wait in silence, or attack."

"He must be really proud," he says. A snowflake of cheese flecks his upper lip. "Probably just doesn't want you to go. Mississippi, where everyone is missed."

I smile because if I don't he'll say *Get it?*

I try to imagine this guy hanging out with my brother, throwing darts or going for a long ride in the truck, his elegant shoes lined with an inch of red Yazoo clay. How easy their talk would be, absent of desire. Do men, who get what they need, know ambition? Back at the house, my sister-in-law and the baby would be hatching plans. A meal for the men, game night, a return to school, finish that nursing degree, a move to New York City, where she could be an ER nurse and the baby could wean itself on Rembrandts at the Met, and at Christmas my brother could visit and everyone would have had their dream.

My proposal has sat unacknowledged on my advisor's desk for six days. I just want a letter saying I'm as functional a human as any other. Is that, as they say, too f-ing much to ask?

"I'll sleep with him," I say, "if it comes to that." Another joke.

Awkward pause. I run through the possible responses: horror, laughter, creepy pressing for details, as if this could turn into a role-play. But he comes to me, through all the walls I've built around him, and places his palm on my forehead.

> *My own, my own,*
> *Who camest to me when the world was gone,*
> *And I who looked for only God, found thee!*
> *I find thee; I am safe, and strong, and glad.*
> *As one who stands in dewless asphodel*
> *Looks backward on the tedious time he had*
> *In the upper life,—so I, with bosom-swell,*
> *Make witness, here, between the good and bad,*
> *That Love, as strong as Death, retrieves as well.*

His palm seems to speak Barrett Browning. Asphodel leaves were once wrapped around burrata because the two expired simultaneously—you could call that effective packaging, or you could call it love.

Asparagus acutefolius, acute-leaved asparagus

A dioecious plant, like asparagus, has split reproductive functions—one plant being male and its neighbor being female. The division takes work; a pollinator with a sense of direction is required. Easier to manage is a monoecious plant, with male and female flowers emerging on a single specimen. Easier still is what is called a perfect flower, with stamens and carpels: hermaphrodite. A world unto itself. You open, you exist, you close.

I know what it is to wait. Better—always—is action.

Ruscus aculeatus, butcher's broom

Deakin, drifting, starts turning plants strangely moralistic. The branches of the *scaccia ragni*—the spider-chase that Italians in black dresses and orthopedic shoes used to sweep away cobwebs—are protective, sweet, maternal. After their berries are borne, they twist their leaves over to shade them. This way the rain doesn't collect beneath the fruit and rot it out. Except, here's a rare advance, Deakin's gang didn't know the leaves weren't leaves at all, but modified stems, cladophylls. Aren't you proud to be living in the twenty-first century? Doesn't it give you a frisson of superiority to know that if you ran into a *Ruscus* on the street, you could shake its shoot and confidently call it a cladode? Isn't that the point of progress, to know more?

To know more *what*?

And to do *what* with it?

I make eggs for breakfast, for him and me, and eat them

all before he wakes. I have fifteen minutes before I need to head out, and I could go brush my dangling hair against his forehead, run my tongue up his arm forest, forgive him again for not being half the things I need. Or I could pull out this postcard I've been saving—cats loose around the Torre Argentina, one bathing himself in the foreground, as feral and innocent as a woman could dream—and address it to my niece.

One day, I write, *I'll tell you all about it.*

Smilax aspera, rough bindweed

In fall the smilax blooms invisibly, with a ferocious, bewildering scent. Before I knew, I would peer into rosebushes, pull apart the dormant jasmine vines. Sweet almonds is what I smelled.

Since I met you, you've inhabited the in-between space each night before sleep, where imagination runs rampant, chokes the native logic. We were in impossible places, your speech impossibly sweet. I used to dream up the next day— and then your letter came. And now I dredge the past.

The nymph Smilax was in love with young Krokos, and something happened, and she died. The gods, taking pity, turned him into a gay spring bulb and her into a vine— black-berried and smelling of carrion, rich with aphrodisiacs and knife-sharp thorns, too lusting to survive a myth.

I start at the beginning each time, my face reflected in your night window, your body smooth and still in the bed. I could imagine it a different way, but I play the scenes by rote, again and again, in faith. Four days left.

A girl on a sill. The action comes.

LXII.

Junceae

Juncus bufonius, toad-rush

The deadline's tomorrow. I'm not an f-ing idiot. I stuff my backpack with notes and pencils (not you-know-who's) and a granola bar so to any night guard I'll look like who I am, a grad student, blind and diligent. I don't believe in ghosts, so I can't say my dead mother is haunting or hounding me, is begging me homeward, to champion some f-ing 1960s mod monstrosity of yellow and white, to raise up the old glory of the Jackson Coliseum as some botanical lodestone. But wouldn't it be nice? Doesn't it serve some kind of justice to pick a new place, to be a new person choosing new things that matter? Not colonizing, but *listening?*

The nights have cooled off, and I've chosen a hat that makes me look either studious or suspicious. I don't know whether the offices are locked at night (probably), but I've got bobby pins in my hair and a credit card in my wallet and a switchblade in my boot. The Iroquois—famous Americans—ate toad rush before a race to vomit themselves light and fast. Faith comes from knowledge, not the other way round. And the only way to get at knowledge is to crack it all the f-ing way open.

LXIII.

Araceae

Arum italicum, Italian cuckoo-pint

The night I received your letter, I appeared to Deakin like a ghost and said, "I can't." I wanted to withdraw from the world. He tried to soothe me; he led me to his chaise. I could hear the mother from a distant room, her snores like bells.

The spadix is a spike of flowers, small, cupped within the spathe's cowl.

He sat me down, put his palm upon my arm, began to stroke. I shrunk into myself. "No," I said, not wanting to be misunderstood. "I can't apprentice."

The lamp lit a drawing he had made, the arum misshapen and the color wrong.

I tried to stand, but my skin caught against his hand. He pulled me down, then pressed me down. "Hush," he said, and with my neck against a pillow, he began undoing buttons. (Mine? His?) My brain seared as my tongue went dumb.

When the spadix falls, the fruit is left: a club of red berries, erect over white-veined leaves.

My buttons? His buttons? Why do women's skirts open at the bottom like bellflowers?

Called lords-and-ladies.

I couldn't speak; I couldn't scream to make his mother wake or the night guards come. All I could say was *no* before my tongue went dumb.

Called bread-of-snakes.

With his weight on top, my limbs awoke. I shoved at his legs with my feet. My elbows thrust into his chest. The lamp threw our shadows like a storm against the wall. He knew my marriage was coming, that I was leaving him. He fought to stop a woman's exit. I fought with my fingernails and my teeth. I could not stop myself from being stolen.

The berries remain *in an oblong crowded spike, after the rest of the plant is decayed.*

The thief must pay.

LXIV.

Cyperaceae

Cyperus, cyperus
C. longus, C. fuscus

The biological sciences department is dark, a single fish in someone's office finning through a fluorescent tank. But the doors are open, as if in some faculty meeting they determined that theft of knowledge should be pardoned. All I hear is my shoes on the linoleum and the soft bubble of the fish trying to breathe.

On the floor behind his desk I find the folder with my proposal, under an article about grasses, above a tabulation of conference expenses. I once asked him when he'd first read Deakin—was it long before he started this project, this recalculation of species—and he laughed and said technically he never had; he was working from the list, of course,

FIG. 10

but the book, with all its extraneous meat—no, he'd never read it. I wanted to quote it to him like poetry—*numerous shining brown, green-keeled glumes*—but that would betray a passion. I wasn't passionate. Or rather I couldn't be, not in his office, couldn't be a woman issuing heat.

I pull the papers, untouched, out of the folder. (Papyrus was a cyperus.) The first question: *How long and in what capacity have you known the applicant?* From my backpack I take my pre-typed answers.

Cyperus, a wetland sedge, can't grow where the water's been leached out of a place. I was a kid when the news was saturated with ozone mania—we made dioramas out of marshmallows showing the hole, and I imagined God peering through the opening we'd made. But now it's something else; the holes are in our soil and water, there are gaps in our species. We learn to live with blanks.

I take the pen from his desk and begin to sign.

Carex depauperata, starved wood-carex

I lift the window from its sill and crawl inside. (I hold that night in my mind, that night always in my mind.) Deakin sleeps, snores, his belly under the down like a heaving sea. I take the papers from his desk, press their edges into a neat stack, fold them into my coat. I am not a woman starved, but swallowing.

LXV.

Gramineae

Phalaris, canary-grass
P. aquatica, P. paradoxa

We're in the grasses now. (I'm either Mowgli or Shere Khan. Someone has a torch.)

Let's break it down: from the roots grows a shoot, which turns into a stalk (or culm), divided into nodes and internodes. From the nodes grow collars and blades. Atop is an inflorescence: spikelets composed of florets (which hide the flowers and soon all the seeds) wearing tails or awns, nestled in two bracts called glumes. The florets look like two holding hands, or like a body riding in a boat, one half called the palea, the other called the lemma.

A lemma is also the word for when you know what you

want to say but don't yet know the word. What you have in your head, inchoate, is a lemma.

Lemma is also Greek for something that is taken. Like hallucinogenics (canary-grass has sent kangaroos staggering, moonstruck, in Australia), or like personal property, or like sex.

Anthroxanthum odoratum, sweet-scented vernal-grass

I send out the invitations with three days left. The night before the marriage will be a dinner: my mother and father and the soldier and Deakin and three acquaintances to round out the tableau. A priest, perhaps, and a neighbor, and an old maid as witness. A feast of vegetables—an offer of gratitude to my recent employer and to the world that made us. (Not you, beloved, all rosy meat.) On the paper I drop homemade perfume. Dried vernal grass, which gives sweet hay its scent, touched with vanilla, as gently as one woman might touch another.

I shine silver for the table and wipe the dust from the crystal rims. I prepare, as all brides, for a crossing.

Alopecurus, foxtail-grass
A. agrestis, A. utriculatus

It's not hard to write yourself a letter of recommendation if you feel wronged. Feeling wronged quite easily stands in for confidence.

Consider the tale of two grasses. One, *A. agrestis*, lives in barren dirt; it creeps along without nutrients, without affection, preferring *poor, exhausted soil* and thus serving as *a natural witness of its ill-conditioned state*. Improve the soil, and the slender foxtail disappears. Let's say this was me. Let's say this is how I was conditioned: to cleave to f-ing shitheads. But its cousin, *A. utriculatus*, likes nice things. It grows in wetness, in fertility. In the Colosseum, it sprouted on the damp north side, *near that arch which is considered to have been the royal entrance*. It aims high. Let's say, optimistically, this is where I want to go. Toward richness, borne not by shitheads or even by men I forgive, but by my own grassy innards.

But you know the end of this. *A. utriculatus* no longer grows in the Colosseum, while *A. agrestis* lasts and lasts. It's always easier to be a natural witness of one's ill-conditioned state.

I have known the applicant for six months, I write, *and can attest that her sight is unparalleled, that her capacity for naming things is strange but necessary.*

Phleum michelii, cat's-tail-grass

Downy glumes, or *hairy*, or *feathery*. You married, I'll marry. We both had our flowers taken. I can't count the years I would've waited for your return. But you wrote the letter that said what women do is moon work, shadow work, pale and uncooked. Greatness is golden, is a lion, and love must have a man. I can name a falsehood when I see it.

Agrostis vulgaris, fine bent grass

My recommendation comes to two pages—glowing, though not suspiciously effusive; she's diligent, she's persistent, she seems to know what the plants are if you give her enough field guides and dichotomous keys. I mention how often she yammers on about Mississippi. The Jackson Coliseum, I make my advisor say, has the potential to reposition the climatic significance of ruderal plant communities. Trash, treasure. The girl is trash; what I can do is make her gold.

On the desk next to his mug of pens and snow globe from Vienna—the mug so misshapen it must have been made by a child (a daughter?) and the globe so unchic someone must've gone out of her way to find something that ugly in Vienna, must have browsed the souvenir racks in the airport with something like vengeance on her mind—next to these is a white golf tee, which certain men keep around like guitar picks, a totem of the kind of person they are. I try to imagine him out there on the clipped grass, likely *A. vulgaris*, beating it repeatedly and aimlessly with a stick. Does he admire the grass's crown? Or on that shorn field does only a man's success matter? The tip of the tee is stained with green.

I scan the recommendation onto university letterhead, the light of the copier like a beacon in the office dark. *I'm on,* it says, *I'm on.* I kiss the mirror of its black plastic. I want to leave my DNA behind.

Piptatherum multiflorum, many-flowered piptatherum

In the dark I'm bodiless. Or just unclothed. In the dark the moon visits, triangulates your face, and my face. I have no desk, so I spread Deakin's papers on the floor. He's revoiced my words. He takes my descriptions of panicle, glumes, awns, and adds agricultural use. Some medicine. With moon-blue ink I cross through what bores me—no farmer reads a flora—and add you. *Loves to locate itself on the tops of old walls and ruins, from whence its long stems and leaves can freely expand on every side, and triumph, in its wild luxuriance, over the destructive work of time, giving that elegant character to them which adds so much of grace even to those which have no feature of beauty of their own, but, drooping over the lofty arches, and hanging in their pendant tufts on those architectural forms of beauty, and massive piles, they add to the wild grandeur of the scene, and seem to be the perennial weepers, with their de-shrivelled forms, mourning over the vast destruction which reigns around them.*

I am making the story anew. You are never absent—deserter, my love—but I must put myself in the center. The language must be mine, and the body.

Lagurus ovatus, hare's-tail-grass

A waste-place grass, my favorite. Its heads are fat and woolly; half call it a weed, and the other half assiduously sow its seeds in overwintering germination pots, under lights, tenderly tending the sprouts till spring, till transplant time. "I LOVE my bunny tails," says online commenter sandrajune from Bohemia, NY.

The point of botany is not to distinguish between value and waste. (There is no waste.) It's to be honest about what something is. A part, a whole, a root, a bloom. Conditions, habits.

Bunnytail is still here, still bopping in the stones that humans cut. It survives Rome's drying climate. Some forty thousand years ago the grasses in Asia began dying, another planetary shift at work, and the *Elasmotherium*—a husky proto-rhinocerous known as the Siberian unicorn—found itself without food. They were made just so: big, heavy, a head hung low, right where the grasses grew. A single horn shot straight out of their skulls. They bore baby unicorns slowly, and the pace of evolution couldn't match the pace of their world changing. The grasses ran out, and the unicorns ate nothing else. They died.

I like to think we would've wanted to keep them, the unicorns, if we'd had a say. Could've made a Unicorn Fund, hosted benefits on yachts. But it was the grasses that mattered. The weeds. And the weeds we cut and strip and shave and vanish.

Koeleria, koeleria
K. cristata, K. phleoides

The seeds were brought in hay. Others came as burrs attached to priests' robes, or stuck in the fur of camels, or caught in the dung of elephants, or hidden in the cheeks of little girls who spit them out at the feet of gladiators at the moment of their martyrdom. Hiding, dropping, waiting, blooming.

Two days before the wedding, and I wash my hands well to erase the ink. I receive a note from Deakin asking have I seen his papers, and I answer that I last saw them being used as fuel by his mother, who could not sleep unless warm. My father says the old man knocks at the door, but I tell him I'm feeling ill, the nerves of an almost-bride, and that I hope to see him tomorrow for the supper. I spread the pages beneath my mattress. In the kitchen I stand with the cook and we begin making jellies.

Avena, oat-grass
A. sterilis, A. fatua, A. hirsuta, A. caryophylla

Standing by a column of gift boxes at the post office with my queue number in my hand, before my daily stakeout at

FIG. II

the Colosseum, I try to put a lid on the voices saying *bad idea, kiddo*. What, the grantees are going to call every recommender and say, "Did you really write what you said you wrote?" Is my advisor going to have a crisis of conscience and then worry that he can no longer find my proposal on his desk? My dead mother once told me, *Truth is all you have*. I had told her I didn't want to go to school because I was sick, then—when I didn't pass the thermometer test—that I didn't want to see Jim McIlhenny, who'd crossed a line. She crossed her eyes. Said, *Truth is all you have*. But what is truth if it's not believed? Nothing. I stopped pointing fingers.

The sterile oat, which hangs its head like all *Avenas*, has an awn that swells and shrinks in response to moisture in the soil, a hygrometer, and it changes so fast it's also called the animated oat—imagine a grass gesturing.

If I can no longer say true things, and am prohibited from saying false things, what the f- is left? *Per gli Stati Uniti*, I say when they call A92, and hand over the envelope. The woman who takes it winks.

Briza, quaking-grass
B. maxima, B. media, B. minor

He floats, a ghost, above the Colosseum. Is he mad or dead? Use all his names: cow-quake, earthquakes, quakers-and-shakers. Doddle-grass, didder, doddering dillies. Jiggle-joggles, jockey-grass, wag-wantons. He's not mad, but quaking—he wakes from his sleep and reads names he didn't write. She robbed his mouth. He howls wide, but no sound comes out. The Colosseum cannot hear the earth shake.

Melica pyramidalis, pyramidal melic-grass

The day before the wedding, I set the table. Fork, cloth mat, knife, spoon. The knife in the middle where it won't leap out. Summer dries into autumn, and all the flowers left are yellow. I stuff a vase with goldenrod, milkwort, and broom. The maid sneezes. The floors have been swept of whatever has not stuck. The candles are lined up, unlit, and the bread left to rise.

In melic grass, the glumelles are unequal, naked, perfect. The ligule—diminutive of *lingua*, tongue—is large, truncated, torn. A glumelle and a ligule in a dance, one hand pressed against the other's back. Candlelight, the smell of bread. One small and nude, the other split in half.

Tonight is the last night. I'll close one passage of my life with a final theft, and on the morrow I'll put my hand in his, a botanist and a soldier, and in the erasure of hope we'll start a new business.

Poa, meadow-grass
P. bulbosa, *P. trivialis*, *P. compressa*, *P. annua*

One of the nastiest, brightest, most tenacious weeds, digging its nails into impossible asphalt and proving ineradicable.

That tuft in the crosswalk? *P. annua*. It's called noxious, which designates a plant as aggressive, as quick to multiply, and as causing adverse effects in humans stupid enough to mess with it. Sounds like a woman, doesn't it?

In England they plant beetle banks, strips of weeds between crop fields where grasses can go apeshit along with bachelor's buttons and sunflowers and borage. The point, I think, is that wiping grasses out makes them madder— better to make a little home for them where birds and bees and all the good things can go, the things that'll pick the pests off your wheat. The birds know what's what; they fatten on noxious seed, nest in injurious crowns.

Eragrostis pilosa, hairy love grass

You can't demand love. Nor expect it, nor wait for it, nor want it. It comes on air like a scent.

Cynosurus, dog's-tail-grass
C. cristatus, *C. echinatus*

The last time I felt it was a week before my dead mother's death. Just us in a room, her on the sofa with a novel, me like a cat on her legs. My eyes smeared with black makeup, as if I knew what was coming, my hair dyed a deep indigo. One pinky nail painted pink, which I kept tucked in my palm so no one would see.

"I wouldn't go if a chariot from hell drove me there," I said. I blew an angry raspberry on her bare knee.

She flipped a page. "What about Sarah?"

"What, we show up arm in arm? Are you fucking serious?"

"Don't say fuck."

"*F-ing?*" I said. "Are you *f-ing* out of your mind?"

"If you wait for a boy to ask," she said, "you've already lost."

I dug my teeth into her skin. She didn't get it *at all*.

"Know what you want before it comes, so you can get it without being gotten. And anyway, you can always count on this much love from me." She spread her hands out, not all the way, but just like she was carrying a round basket. It seemed reasonably sized at the time, not epic.

I went to the dance with my best friend and we were called lesbians by the cheerleaders, who held one another's bare legs all day, and we took photos with our middle fingers out. If you collect a hundred silky long-tailed awns—sweet, bending—into a single inflorescence, they make not a bouquet but a club.

Dactylis glomerata, rough cock's-foot-grass

The gatekeeper feeds on cock's foot. A gatekeeper is a moth, orange, with two brown eyes. A gatekeeper is a man who writes the science, or a priest who makes the mass, or a father who lays down the law. But tonight it is me and the maid and my mother in the kitchen, stirring sauce and pressing the potatoes and cutting off the heads of brussels sprouts, making the meal, making the gate.

Bromus, brome-grass
B. racemosus, B. mollis, B. arvensis, B. aspera,
B. sterilis, B. madritensis, B. maximus

Brome's another unwanted one, and, Deakin swears, is *refused by almost all cattle.* Almost! My storymaking brain jumps to the one experimental cow who sees the golden light hitting the seedheads in late afternoon and, starved, thinks, *Tasty!* Deakin's angry, he's working up to something, he calls the panicle *erect, stiff, dilated, swollen.* I know a little something about a mad scientist.

He finds me in the Colosseum, a couple weeks after the office heist; I'm on my knees in the dirt pulling at the internodes of grasses in search of telltale ligules, and he stands there with a manila folder in his hand, blocking the sun, intentionally (I'm sure) Hitchcockian. I wait for him to slap the folder against his palm, for added effect.

"I was impressed with your proposal," he says.

I want to say how totally not possible that is, given that it doesn't exist anywhere he can reach, unless he's a secret postal employee on the weekends. I also want to say how being "impressed" is not something a man like him feels toward women, how all of this is such an f-ing lie, such a blatant setup.

"I'm meeting some folks for lunch," he waves his hand in the direction of the real world, the non-Colosseum, where modern people eat and converse and keep their knees clean, "but do you want to swing by the office tonight and we'll chat?"

Oh yeah, I think, *sure thing I'll swing by. I adore getting called out on my lies, love getting disciplined by a man twice my age.*

"I have a date tonight," I say. I've sexualized it—*boom*—and I regret it.

Festuca, fescue-grass
F. rigida, F. myurus, F. pseudo-myurus,
F. romana, F. ovina, F. segetum

I came to a place in the flora that I could not erase. Beneath my careful delineations of panicle, spikelets, awn, and roots, Deakin composed an ode to the Roman sheep. Can a villain too have precious thoughts? Are there lines to be drawn between waste and worth?

In the last hour before supper I take a turn at the stew. The stirring keeps it whole.

Elymus europaeus, European lyme-grass

I go anyway. It's August-hot in November, and the man I forgave left a voicemail (*I found something you'll want to see, you'll really like*), but I don't want to want, I want to be brave. Is this what they mean by *asking for trouble?* No, it's insisting on victory. We lose until we win.

A third-floor window in the science building is lit up; someone is moving books from one shelf to another in such an uninterrupted rhythm that I assume it's a woman, and start guessing what pitch my screams will need to be to reach her. These are a soldier's thoughts.

It's nearly impossible to tell lyme-grass from barley, *Hordeum*. One of those species that shouldn't have its own genus, and sure enough, *Elymus* eventually became *Hordelymus*, which is to say, *I guess this is basically barley?* There are lines between things, and lines between acts. This is me; this is you. This is love; this is theft. Definition upholds sanity.

In the basement, the lamp turns his face green, fishy. His eel tongue pokes around the mustache's detritus. The desk is a city of manila folders; I don't know how he ever found mine gone. A mug of coffee steams in the underwater light, this mug also messily made. I point to it. "Kids?"

He hunches over the steam till his glasses fog, and then he takes them off. We are playing truth poker.

"I got a call from my friend Bernard."

I nod, as if I too have Bernards in my life.

"He said the committee was surprised to see I was recommending this sort of project."

Hordeum, barley
H. murinum, H. pratense

He arrives red-cheeked, demands in a whisper to see me. My father tells him I'm finishing the garnishes, ushers him to the soldier. The men shake hands. From the kitchen I hear my tomorrow-husband saying gentle things; there will be no scene tonight.

Behind the jar of flour on the shelf above the stove I've hidden my bridal pouch. Twenty-four leaves of dog's mercury. The recipe won't need them all.

Hordeum refers to the hairy inflorescence, from the Latin *horrere*, to bristle. *Horrere* being also the root of *horror*. To bristle.

Gaudinia fragilis, brittle-gaudinia

So brittle that it's gone, at least from this dust bowl, which in better days one historian called *a giant stone vase*. How easy, to eliminate something living from the earth. As simple as turning up the temperature, or slipping a pill in a drink, or touching a leg, or doubting.

I say I'm sorry but the funding was important, and I had no reason to believe he'd have helped.

"No, I wouldn't have," he says.

"Yes, *why*."

"It isn't a smart project."

"What makes this Colosseum better than another?"

"History," he says. "This is the seventh flora. Knowledge is built over time."

"That's so obviously not true," I say, very much intending not to cry. "People like you need to duplicate things because you don't have the f-ing guts to start them."

"People like me?" He takes the mug when he stands and comes over to my side of the desk. I see it slow-motion, him pouring the coffee on my lap, but he doesn't. He takes a sip, sets it down, his standing leg hard against my sitting one. He leans forward and puts a hand, warm from the mug, somewhere between my shoulder and my neck. It feels like he's feeling for my pulse. I breathe as quiet as a rabbit, all my intentions to scream shrunk into self-preservation. If I breathe so quiet, I think, he won't see that I'm here.

Triticum, wheat-grass
T. villosum, T. repens

We bring the bread on platters, my mother and the maid and I. We fill the glasses with wine. The men admire the pattern of potatoes, and Deakin is soothed by the stew.

"How is it to lose a daughter?" he asks.

Does he think of what he made me lose?

My father wipes the cream from the corners of his mouth. "A relief!"

The men laugh. The wine makes the women's presence palatable.

For dessert I've made the puddings in small porcelain cups, each wearing its own corsage. A yellow sow thistle, a pink scabious, violet harebells, a white cyclamen hanging like a shepherd's crook above the chocolate mousse. The soldier says how charming.

"I picked them from the Colosseum."

"The best of botany!" my father says. A girl putting flowers on food.

I let the soldier rest his hand on mine for a moment before I reach for a spoon. The *Mercurialis perennis* leaves on Deakin's mousse look like mint; he doesn't recognize them. He hasn't done the work, so he's missing all the signs. (*There's wit in every flower, if you can gather it.*) In the vase of autumn grass at the table's center springs a dried stem of *Triticum*: common couch, twitch, quick grass, dog grass, witch grass.

Brachypodium, false brome-grass
B. sylvaticum, B. pinnatum, B. distachyon

The only false brome left is *B. distachyon*, the smallest, fastest-growing, the weediest. Even its genome is small, making it perfect for fiddling scientists to breed and map and molest.

He lifts his hand from my skin as intently as he put it there, straightens his leg so our knees no longer touch.

"I admire your enthusiasm," he says, circling his desk again, again putting the green light between us. It's the wrong word. *Desperation* would be closer. "But I told Bernard your letter was forged."

Yes, *forged*. Made, like steel, like a bond. I made it.

"They've disqualified your application."

A twitch is running along my left side, from my heart to my foot, like a sound wave. *Yes*, I want to say, *but are you going to hurt me?*

Aegilops ovata, ovate spiked hard-grass

There was a night, after I first met you and before you said goodbye, when I was young and you were young and the walls were short around your father's house, and under a nursery moon we climbed through the window, you apprenticing on my heels, and down the vines and across the stone pavings, dusty with straw and shit, and over—like water— over the dam. You in a green robe, stem-colored. We became part of the night public.

I've had dreams where we never came back.

The Sicilian peasantry, it is said, gather it when ripe, and tie the heads up into bunches, and set them on fire.

Grasses set flower and grasses die, and the flowering

doesn't prevent the death, and the death doesn't disprove the flame.

Lolium, darnel
L. perenne, L. multiflora

Deakin tells me there's a third darnel, *L. temulentum*, that can f- people up. He takes a weird amount of time in a passage about the other innocuous darnels to let me know *really, watch out* about a plant that never even grew in the Colosseum. As if the Colosseum were a game we both were playing, but actually he's leaning in and describing the whole f-ing terrifying world out there. *The only known species of grass that produces . . . fatal effects.*

The *Loliums* are still here, because no one wants them.

What do you want me to do, Deakin? Isn't the weed's greatest—its only—strength refusing to die?

Earlier today, before this leg-on-leg nightmare, I forwarded my flight info to my brother, who texted back faster than normal. The counseling sessions are working; these days, his gratitude sweatily clambers over his fear. There's a holiday photo circulating of his family in matching tartan.

"We'll do it right, make her lasagna."

"That lasagna was dry as bones," I texted.

"Baby's first Christmas. She has to learn about her grandma."

"And a million other things."
Weeds that bend live forever.

Tragus racemosus, branched tragus

He begins to pull at his throat, a childish gesture, as if something were stuck there and he could grasp it from the outside. The men are in the smoking room, dark and red, and the women have moved the empty plates and porcelain cups to the kitchen, where some will break. In the hallway I stand next to the table where your letter once lay, burning.

Through the door I catch his claws reaching up to his ears. They flame away from his face. Seeds are hidden in burrs so they stick. Life doesn't replicate without pain. His lower jaw swells; the man who'll be my groom tomorrow kneels beside him, beats Deakin's chest with a fist. I wonder what you do with your husband. His legs begin to twitch, and my father presses against the other man's thighs, as if slowing them will save them. Men with their hands on one another's bodies. One of Deakin's eyes finds me; I wave in the haze of his vision, grass in the doorway. He begins to tire, the redness of his face fading, a fleck of foam at his tongue.

"Water!" the soldier shouts.

The women move around me with palliatives. I have his book in my room; I have my own book. His eyelids dip. I cannot help seeing in his stead a plant, reactive, mimosa-sensitive, shuddering. I am stealing his breath. Thieves beget theft. A dose of dog's mercury, and *the victim turns blue as he dies.*

Setaria, bristle-grass
S. verticillata, S. viridis

Without the green light, his office turns blue. It comes from the moon, or is born of darkness.

"That's all," he says.

Now he's in his chair and I'm standing. I think of what I could tell the dean, my committee, the police. *After I committed academic fraud, a man briefly put his leg against my leg.* How small was the office? *The office was small.* It could've been an accident. Did he touch your breasts? *He ended my career.* Did you falsify a letter of recommendation for a funding proposal? *Yes, but—* What was it for? To go home? Were you homesick? *No, it was to put myself in science.* Science has survived for so long without you. *There were 420 species of plants growing in the Colosseum in 1855, and now there are 242. Don't tell me what's surviving.* What now? You want to press charges?

The teeth on the bristle grass are backward, the hooks turning inward, because to catch something you've got to first be facing yourself.

I leave his office to the man and the moon. My dead mother once held a snapdragon to my face and growled, *No one listens to monsters.* If I had a daughter, I'd correct the error. Holding up a crown of foxtail, I'd whisper, *Everyone listens to monsters, but they can be slain; weeds go on and on and on and on and on.*

Cynodon dactylon, creeping dog's-tooth-grass

They take the body out of my father's house and I sleep on a flora as another woman might sleep on violets and with my window open and the air resting its palm on my cheek I conjure you, your leafed fingers and your corolla nose, and you don't touch me—so in the morning I wake and wear my bridal dress, its pouch shaken empty, and under a colorless drizzle I step into a church and give my body to a man who takes lives for a living and when he kisses me at last I am unmoved and this is the way things grow, toward light and away.

LXVI.

Filices

Polypodium vulgare, polypody

He floats, a vulgar ghost, above the Colosseum. Nothing tethers him; soon he'll vanish. He made love, and she made his white face blue. If he'd had the fern, the *"rheum-purging Polypody"* of *Shakespear* (she wrote), he would have spit out his last apologia through the choke: *I wanted not you but to master my mortality.* But now his book is hers, and the earth boils him to vapor.

Adiantum capillus veneris, true maiden-hair

Maidenhair is still here, of course—the last genus on the list.

"That one?" asks the man I forgave, pointing to the

spade-shaped leaves falling from the wall like ponytails. "Those are in Jackson too?"

I pinch the webbing between his thumb and forefinger. "I don't have the money anymore."

"Seems like a fairly low-tech project."

"It's not like— You can't just make up science. You have to be attached to something, some kind of academic structure, or a research center or something."

"Is that what your hero Deakin did?"

Saying *he's not my hero* would make me sound six years old.

But listen: *pale, membranous, reflexed; long, black, wiry and fibrous; quite smooth, shining, brittle; the lower half naked.*

"I'm listening," he says. "I'd go wherever your brain goes."

I shake my head. "It's going too far," I say. "It's orbiting."

Maidenhair drapes the Fountain of Egeria, where the emperors went to learn the way from women, and where women went to steal some space for themselves, to try to figure their f-ing lives out. We're given nothing freely; we have to cut and carve what we need.

I dig a sprong of fern from the wall and stash it in my backpack, bound for home. Time will tell if it survives.

I never see the man again.

FIG. 12

Asplenium trichomanes, wall-spleenwort

A remembrance fern grows anywhere. Without light, on graves. The spores are held in sori, black spots beneath the fingered leaves, and—according to him, or me—*as they expand, become confluent*. Their stories run together. The weeds outlive the narrative.

I finish the book and let them publish it under his name.

In the summer I have a daughter.

LIST OF PLATES,
FLORA COLISEA MISSISSIPPIANA

FIG. 1:   *Vitis labrusca*, fox grapevine
FIG. 2:   *Viola sororia*, common blue violet
FIG. 3:   *Daucus carota*, Queen Anne's lace
FIG. 4:   *Solidago altissima*, tall goldenrod
FIG. 5:   *Silybum marianum*, milk thistle
FIG. 6:   *Lonicera japonica*, Japanese honeysuckle
FIG. 7:   *Physostegia virginiana*, obedient plant
FIG. 8:   *Datura stramonium*, jimsonweed
FIG. 9:   *Tipularia discolor*, crane-fly orchid
FIG. 10: *Carex grayi*, Gray's sedge
FIG. 11: *Chasmanthium latifolium*, river oats
FIG. 12: *Onoclea sensibilis*, sensitive fern

FLORA COLISEA

Panaroli, *Plantarum Amphytheatralium Catalogus*, 1643

Sebastiani, *Enumeratio plantarum sponte nascentium in ruderibus Amphiteatri Flavii*, 1815

Deakin, *Flora of the Colosseum of Rome*, 1855

Fiorini Mazzanti, *Florula del Colosseo*, 1874

Anzalone, "Flora e vegetazione dei muri di Roma," 1951

Celesti Grapow et al., "La Flora del Colosseo (Roma)," 2001

AUTHOR'S NOTE

I am indebted to Richard Deakin's *Flora of the Colosseum of Rome*, which is liberally quoted here, always in italics, and also to Giulia Caneva et al., "Analysis of the Colosseum's Floristic Changes During the Last Four Centuries," *Plant Biosystems* 136, no. 3 (2002). Other italicized quotations come from the Bible; Elizabeth Barrett Browning, "Sonnet 27 (My Own Belovèd, Who Hast Lifted Me)"; Committee on Women in Science, Engineering, and Medicine, "Consensus Study Report Highlights," based on the National Academy of Sciences' "Sexual Harassment of Women: Climate, Culture, and Consequences in Academic Science, Engineering, and Medicine" (2018); John Donne, "A Fever"; John Gerard, *Herbal* (1597); Ferdinand Gregorovius, *History of the City of Rome in the Middle Ages* (1859–72); Emily S. Gurley et al., "Fatal Outbreak from Consuming *Xanthium strumarium* Seedlings During Time of Food Scarcity in Northeastern Bangladesh," *PLOS One* 5, no 3 (2010); Horace, "Ode 1.31"; John Jacob, *West Devon and Cornwall Flora* (1836); Mae Jemison, from "Then & Now: Dr. Mae Jemison," CNN.com,

June 19, 2005; John Keats, "Ode to a Nightingale"; Gerald McCarthy, "Botany as a Disciplinary Study," *Journal of the Elisha Mitchell Scientific Society* 6, no. 1 (1889); John Mc-Crae, "In Flanders Field"; sandrajune, "I LOVE my bunny tails," DavesGarden.com, June 20, 2018; Percy Bysshe Shelley, "The Sensitive Plant"; James Shirley, *The Gentleman of Venice* (1655); Weeds Act 1959 (UK); Eudora Welty, 1945 letter to John Robinson, quoted in Julia Eichelberger's *Tell about Night Flowers: Eudora Welty's Gardening Letters, 1940–1949* (2013); and William Wordsworth, "To the Daisy (Third Poem)." I also acknowledge the abundant utility of Wikipedia in bringing me closer to plants I didn't have the opportunity to see.

All my gratitude to MacDowell, the Residency Program at the Dora Maar House, and the Santa Maddalena Foundation, three places where I found time, friendship, and new weeds. Thank you also to Stefan Block; Rob Ferguson; Rien Fertel; Rebecca Dinerstein Knight; Victoria Ramírez Mansilla; Sarah Phillips; Simon Smith; Steve Smith; Samantha D'Acunto and the New York Botanical Garden's Mertz Library; Nicolle Jordan and the *Southern Quarterly*, which published an excerpt of the work-in-progress; Kathy Schermer-Gramm; Bill Clegg; Jenna Johnson; and my own gardening mother, who is luckily still alive.

A Note About the Author

Katy Simpson Smith was born and raised in Jackson, Mississippi. She is the author of the novels *The Story of Land and Sea*, a *Vogue* best book of the year; *Free Men*; and *The Everlasting*, a *New York Times* best historical fiction book of the year. She is also the author of *We Have Raised All of You: Motherhood in the South, 1750–1835*. Her writing has appeared in *The Paris Review*, the *Los Angeles Review of Books*, the *Oxford American*, *Granta*, and *Literary Hub*, among other publications. She received a PhD in history from the University of North Carolina at Chapel Hill and an MFA from the Bennington Writing Seminars. She lives in New Orleans.